A Glasshouse of Stars

Also by Shirley Marr

YOUNG ADULT
Fury
Preloved

MIDDLE GRADE
Little Jiang

A Glasshouse of Stars

SHIRLEY MARR

Simon & Schuster Books for Young Readers
NEW YORK   LONDON   TORONTO   SYDNEY   NEW DELHI

SIMON & SCHUSTER BOOKS FOR YOUNG READERS
An imprint of Simon & Schuster Children's Publishing Division
1230 Avenue of the Americas, New York, New York 10020

This book is a work of fiction. Any references to historical events, real people, or real places are used fictitiously. Other names, characters, places, and events are products of the author's imagination, and any resemblance to actual events or places or persons, living or dead, is entirely coincidental.

For information about special discounts for bulk purchases, please contact Simon & Schuster Special Sales at 1-866-506-1949 or business@simonandschuster.com.
The Simon & Schuster Speakers Bureau can bring authors to your live event. For more information or to book an event, contact the Simon & Schuster Speakers Bureau at 1-866-248-3049 or visit our website at www.simonspeakers.com.
Interior design by Hilary Zarycky
The text for this book was set in Arrus.
Manufactured in the United States of America
0521 FFG
First Edition
2   4   6   8   10   9   7   5   3   1
Library of Congress Cataloging-in-Publication Data
Names: Marr, Shirley, author.
Title: A glasshouse of stars / Shirley Marr.
Description: First edition. | New York : Simon & Schuster Books for Young Readers, [2021] | Based on the author's childhood experiences. | Audience: Ages 8–12. | Audience: Grades 4–6. | Summary: Inheriting First Uncle's home after he dies tragically and unexpectedly, eleven-year-old Meixing and her family immigrate to the New Land, where it will take all of Meixing's resilience and bravery to finally find her place of belonging in this new world.
Identifiers: LCCN 2020050888 (print) | LCCN 2020050889 (ebook) | ISBN 9781534488830 (hardcover) | ISBN 9781534488854 (ebook)
Subjects: CYAC: Emigration and immigration—Fiction. | Immigrants—Fiction. | Resilience (Personality trait)—Fiction. | Belonging (Social psychology)—Fiction. | Culture shock—Fiction.
Classification: LCC PZ7.1.M37265 Gl 2021 (print) | LCC PZ7.1.M37265 (ebook) | DDC [Fic]—dc23
LC record available at https://lccn.loc.gov/2020050888
LC ebook record available at https://lccn.loc.gov/2020050889

A Glasshouse of Stars

CHAPTER ONE

House

You have arrived for a better life at the New House in the New Land. It has been a long journey, the first time you've ever been on an airplane. It was nerve-racking when they checked the suitcases at the airport, even though your family has next to no possessions, let alone anything to hide. You didn't know what big meant until you saw the city with the glass towers that touched the sky, the suburbs with houses so close together. You tell yourself everything is going to be fine. The hardest part is over. You made it.

You're all too scared to go inside. First Uncle could be in there. He insisted on a funeral as per the local customs of this land—one that possibly didn't include the ritual of telling him he was now *dead*, so he might have come home unaware.

Ma Ma's knuckles are white from grasping the

yellow protective talisman with both hands. Ba Ba pretends superstitions are for ignorant people. He inserts the key into the door. He doesn't turn the handle.

The rag doll that Ma Ma made out of an old rice sack is clasped tightly in your arms—you are much too old for her anymore, but she's all you have. You stare up at the huge white columns propping up the crumbly tofu triangle of a roof. The long drop down to earth from the winding stone staircase you have climbed creates the same scary feeling in your stomach.

You turn instinctively toward Ma Ma's side as you used to do, to bury your face inside the folds of her dress. But now that she is huge with child, she has taken to gently nudging you away, so you pull away before she does.

"I didn't expect it to be . . . a mansion," says Ma Ma.

"Houses in the New Land are all supposed to be big. I have been warned," replies Ba Ba.

You stare up, disorientated. You don't know if the house is truly too big or if it's only big because you're used to living in a cramped space.

Long fingers of cactus reach all the way up to the second floor, covering the walls like hands on a face. Balanced on the roof at the very top is a third story, a single room with a semicircular window like an open eye.

A light inside the window flickers on and then off again. A wink. No, it is just your imagination. But what a strange thing to imagine. You look over at your parents, but they don't seem to have noticed.

The cold winter wind blows, an icy chill that none of you have ever felt before. The amber pane in the middle of the front door is frosted and blind. Ba Ba rattles at the handle, which appears to be stuck. Suddenly, it gives way and you all tumble into a musty darkness.

It takes your eyes a while to adjust. Soon you realize you are staring at a world made completely out of dark brown wood and motes of dust that float past your nose like magic.

Ba Ba turns the hallway light on, and everything is a yellow glow. He takes the talisman off Ma Ma and sticks it outside, above the front doorframe, where the wind flaps it all about. You think the protection spell written on it is for babies, because magic is childish, but you are relieved all the same.

Inside the house, on the brown brick wall facing the entrance, Ba Ba places an octagon with a piece of mirror in the middle called a *bagua*. To reflect bad luck away. Later he will go outside, light incense sticks, and thank First Uncle for your new home.

Ma Ma is told to go straight to the bedroom and have a lie-down, even though she protests. She says she will have time enough to rest after the baby is born, because for a whole month Ma Ma will not be allowed to do anything. Not even have a shower, even if she complains her hair is oily or her armpits are stinky, not one.

The only thing she will be allowed to do after the birth is rest. Your Aunties told you that there is nothing more important than looking after the baby—and why would Ma Ma want to be doing anything else, anyway? That, and the fact that Ma Ma has to eat lots of stewed pork knuckle. Ginger and sweet black vinegar, too, but mostly pork knuckle.

This is how things are. Like the *bagua* on the wall. Like the fact your parents seem much more relieved now that the *bagua* is up. Like the fact you have come to this New Land to start a new and better life. You don't question it.

You have to be a good girl.

Free to explore by yourself, you find the kitchen is completely orange. The bathroom is lime green. The rest of the house, though, is that dark wooden brown. You don't think these are the prettiest colors in the world, but they're the colors New House is, and you are determined to get along. Because when you look down at your skin, you know it is darker than the people in this New Land, and when you see the plait of hair over your shoulder, you know nobody here has coarse black hair like yours. Maybe you look frightening and different.

"I'm sorry you didn't get to meet First Uncle," says Ba Ba. "It would have been nice to all live together. There's definitely the space for it."

He has a newspaper open and is struggling to read beyond the meager handful of words he knows.

"Can you understand this?" he asks.

LABORER NEEDED

NO EXPERIENCE REQUIRED

You shake your head. You become aware that you haven't said anything since this morning, when you realized it was the day to get onto the plane and leave your old home forever. You get the sinking feeling you're going to find it hard to talk much again.

The words are too big anyway, and the only word you can read (which is "no") doesn't help at all. Ba Ba rubs his chin. You are both in the same boat. Ba Ba gives up and turns the page to see if anything makes more sense on the other side, but it is the same story.

Now that you have seen everything down here, you are determined to go upstairs.

You think of that window.

It blinked once at you.

Perhaps if you find the room, you might find the eye and the face and the part of the giant behind it, looking through the entire house like a camera. Maybe this house was built by giants. That would explain why it's so big; otherwise, why would First Uncle have all this space for one person?

"Don't wander too far, Meixing," your father calls. "I might need you for something else."

New House has lots of different tiles—small multicolored patchwork in one bathroom, white with yellow daisies in another bathroom, and brown-and-orange circles in the kitchen. Everywhere else, uneven squares the color of baked earth undulate and shift like sand. The house wears all of them like scales.

Tiles are something you are used to. The tiny apartment you lived in was made of white uniform tiles that were everywhere, even the bedrooms.

"Fit for the hot weather. Easy to sweep," Ma Ma had said.

Upstairs, though, there is something strange on

the floor. Shaggy, spongy, and dirty, with round patches of dark burgundy here and there. This, you presume, is New House's fur; the marks, her spots.

You stretch out and place your bare foot on top, trapping the fibers in between your toes. You don't know what you were expecting, perhaps a growl. Instead, you feel a vibration. It could be your imagination, it could be the house settling, it could be a purr.

First Uncle has made a bedroom for you, but it is only half finished because he had a heart attack while picking oranges out in the backyard, one week before you were all to arrive—this is the awful news First Uncle's lawyer told Ba Ba. This is why only one of the walls is painted. One perfect pink square, like a sheet of joss paper.

But you have your *own* bedroom.

You no longer all have to sleep together, two mattresses on the floor pushed together like an ill-fitting puzzle. Feet against head, head against feet.

In comparison, New House is a palace. You should feel like a princess, but you instead feel more like an intruder who might at any moment be told to go back home. You place your rag doll on the bed, with the superstitious worry that it will be rejected by some unwritten rule of this inner universe. Nothing happens to the doll. She slumps against the pillow and you are relieved.

As if sensing that you need a distraction, a door creaks somewhere beyond your bedroom. This prompts you to go out and investigate. The house appears to watch you as you wander down the hall and find a pale pink door you swear you didn't pass before. You stick your head inside.

The ceiling in this room is not in line with the height of the other ceilings. It is three times as tall, to fit what you discover is an entire playground complete with a rocket, a slide, and a spinning wheel. It is too much.

You run away in fright and bolt back down the hallway. You stop at your bedroom door, your hand over your heart. It is beating like mad. How big is this house? How scary?

Big Scary.

The house slowly closes the door you have left open; the creaking sound, a sad whimper.

"It's not your fault you're scary, but it's not my fault I'm scared," you whisper to the house, the first words you have said all day.

There is a tapping noise along the hallway. Big Scary is composing a long response.

"If you're angry about me being here, know that I wish I wasn't here either."

You shut your bedroom door behind you and sit cross-legged on the bed, staring out the window into the backyard. You see waist-high weeds and a broken-down house made of glass. You don't see any orange trees. The orange trees were all First Uncle ever talked about in his letters and on the phone. About watering and pruning and what type of animal poo was the best and when and how to apply it.

On the fence sits a black-and-white cat, wondering if she is brave enough to jump down into that long, wild grass. She looks at you and you look back at her. She winks and then jumps back to the safe side of the fence she came from. You rub your eyes in surprise, and then you rub them again. Looking all around you with blurred vision at these strange new surroundings, you wish you could jump back to safety too.

CHAPTER TWO

Noodles

After a while, once you have tucked all your feelings back inside where they belong, you resume your mission to explore. You circle the entire second floor, but you can't find a door that takes you up to the Room on the Roof. The pink door with the rocket behind it has been hastily withdrawn, and you cannot find it again. That makes you deeply sad because you hate seeing things leave you, even if you never liked or wanted them in the first place.

You touch the wall and the wall touches you back. You pull away in surprise. Taking a step backward, you almost fall down a small spiral staircase. This little secret takes you round and round all the way downstairs, to the door of your parents' bedroom. You wonder why this staircase exists—if it is to connect children to their parents, why do they have to be so far apart in the first place?

"Did you go exploring? What do you think?" Ma Ma asks as you climb into her bed.

You don't reply. You want to snuggle underneath her arm, but you are too afraid to touch her—not with her swollen feet and sweaty, irritable personality prone to suddenly changing from glad to mad, as if controlled by the mystery force growing inside her. Your arms wouldn't be able to wrap all the way around her anymore, anyway.

"How do you feel?" Ma Ma asks.

You feel nervous, upside down, inside out, heart in your mouth, snakes in your stomach, intimidated, and scared. But you don't say so, in case the fear crawls out of your mouth and takes the form of monsters. Not of the type that can be repelled by Ba Ba's *bagua*, but of the realities of new people and new places and an unknown future.

"I would like that pony I saw on the TV at the airport," you whisper instead.

You are thinking of that soft plastic horse with the rainbow hair, the one that smells like strawberries and can be any color as long as you like pastel. The cargo ship that used to arrive at your island every three months (and not at all during the typhoon season) only ever brought boring things like food and basic supplies. You made your own toys with matchboxes, bottle caps, and rubber bands looped together to form a skipping rope. Ma Ma cut up an old cotton rice bag and sewed the white bits together to make your rag doll, the colored bits into her dress. You never named her.

"Of course," Ma Ma replies with a laugh. "Now we are starting our lives fresh over, we can have anything we want."

"What do you want?" you ask Ma Ma timidly.

"Well, I would really like one of those brand-new kitchen appliances that can turn from a mixer to a blender to a grinder. Imagine how much of a whiz I'd become in the kitchen!"

You both laugh as you remember the time Ba Ba had gifted Ma Ma with a new electric eggbeater, only for Ma Ma to still use her old metal whisk. You are glad to see Ma Ma can be the funny person here that she was back home.

"I don't really need a magic kitchen appliance," says Ma Ma. "All I want is for us to be happy in our new home. For everything to be wonderful."

She reaches over and finally engulfs you in a hug, and you remember how things used to be; you love her so much. And one day you might learn to love the baby in her tummy, like you've been told you have to, even though right now it is an abstract, unformed idea in your head.

The doorbell rings. You both stare at each other in surprise. No one knows you're here. You have no friends. Know not a single soul.

Ba Ba has already opened the door by the time you've raced over. A woman and man stand on the tattered doormat. The woman is holding a tower of plastic containers, which she passes awkwardly over to your father.

"Huynh," the man says. He points to himself and his wife.

"Lim," replies Ba Ba, patting his chest. He puts his hand on your head.

"Aunty. Uncle," you say politely. They are not related to you, of course, you've only just met them, but it is custom for you to call anyone older than you by these names as a sign of respect.

Mr. Huynh takes a step back and points over to the single-level, brown-brick house next door, to the left of Big Scary. "Home."

"Please, come in," says Ba Ba. He is careful to enunciate the New Language carefully.

"So, this is the food everyone eats in this coun try?" you whisper to your father in the Old Languag There are rice noodles in one of the clear boxes, aromatic beefy flavor coming from it. You think y can smell coriander and mint.

13

"No, not exactly . . . ," replies Ba Ba. "They are more like us."

This only confuses you. You're sure they haven't come from the same place you did. This is not a dish that Ma Ma cooks.

In the kitchen Ba Ba points to the ad in the newspaper, and Mr. Huynh says, "Work," then mimes lifting something heavy off the ground. No one can understand his charade. So he uses the phone on the wall to call the number and speaks to the person on the other end in a pause-and-go staccato, but it is much better New Language than you are capable of.

Ma Ma comes out of the bedroom. She looks tired, one hand on the small of her back, one cupped underneath that giant belly. There are so many questions you have for Ma Ma. Who are these people who are neither the Old People nor the New People? What is this food that is similar to what she cooks, but not the same; what is anything anymore? But she sees you open your mouth and, as if she fears what might come out, quickly looks away and out the window. You feel her emotionally pull away from everyone, even you.

There is a kind pressure on your arm, and Mrs. Huynh leads you away and walks around the house with you. She takes you into the formal dining room,

where there sits a huge wooden table with legs that end in cat's paws. She points at the ancestral photos on the walls. You have no idea who any of these people are, just that they all look unhappy. The unhappiest of all is the beautiful bride in the black-and-white wedding picture.

Mrs. Huynh smiles and takes your chin in her hand.

"Son. No friend," she says to you. She tries to gesture with her hands, but the meaning doesn't come out. She clicks her tongue at herself. You are lost with each other and lost in this land.

As they are leaving, the Huynhs invite you all over to their place. Ma Ma declines and says maybe tomorrow. Through the sliver of the closing bedroom door, you watch as Ma Ma lies down and stares up at the ceiling. Then you follow Ba Ba next door.

The house is really small, uniformly brown, and does not appear to be alive like your house. It is also extremely cluttered. Nothing is thrown out, not even empty boxes or the newspapers stacked up high, slowly turning into fossils.

Ba Ba and Mr. Huynh go out back to look at something. You sit down in front of the television on a neon green and black leopard-print rug, which you definitely expect to be alive, but it is not.

The news is playing, and you learn of a civil war happening in a faraway place called Lebanon, but it does not look civil at all. There is also a cold war between two countries, but it seems heated and rash instead. A shuttle blasts into space and a woman prime minister gives a speech. Mrs. Huynh gets up and switches the channel.

You watch a cartoon about a princess of power who holds a glittering magic sword high up in the air. Mrs. Huynh sits behind you in the armchair, sewing buttons on a huge stack of clothes that appear too big to belong to either of them. There is a large jar of buttons and a large jar of coins on either side of her.

There is a feeling that you are being watched. You quickly turn your head, and something comes crashing down, but whatever or whoever it was has disappeared from the doorway. You keep watching and, sure enough, a hand comes creeping around the corner to retrieve the dropped toy spaceship. You watch for a little while longer, but the rest of the body that belongs to the hand does not show itself.

You go back to watching that colorful cartoon. Mrs. Huynh stares at the empty doorway, shakes her head, and clicks her tongue again. After you leave the house, you are still left wondering about the owner of that mystery hand.

First Uncle must not have cooked much at home, as both the pantry and the fridge prove to be bare. Ma Ma unpacks the noodle dish from Mrs. Huynh with suspicion and gives it a good sniff. Your parents won't eat the noodle dish because they don't eat beef. But they say you can because you are in the New Land now. When you point out that they are part of the New Land too, they laugh and say that they are too old for some things to change. Ma Ma and Ba Ba share a rice dish instead. You push the mound of raw mint, bean sprouts, and chiles aside, but you eat everything else. The meal is delicious. You tell yourself some new experiences are good.

That night, lying in the secondhand pink-framed bed that First Uncle bought for you, your parents feel a whole universe away downstairs. Your rag doll, with her one-dimensional drawn-on face, provides no comfort. The pink wall, softly glowing in the dark, is keeping you awake. You still haven't found the way to the Room on the Roof. It has been a really long day. You have traveled thousands of miles over the ocean, and your stomach still feels as though it's up in the air.

The wardrobe door creaks open. You pull your covers closer to your face. Maybe it's your imagination, but a slice of neon pink glows out of that crack.

Out of bed and you are fleeing down the stairs with your hair standing on end, so fast that it feels as if you're flying. You dive under the blanket between the two sleeping bodies of your parents, and when they wake and ask you what's wrong, you don't want to tell them. Ma Ma groans and tosses in bed. She tries tucking another pillow between her knees, but now that she is awake, she cannot get comfortable again. She gets up and pads to the kitchen.

The light that reaches the bedroom is normal and yellow. You relax back into your parents' bed, although you refuse to take the blanket off your face. The more you think about it, the less sense it makes—what would be haunting your room? A pink monster?

There are real things you ought to be scared of, you remind yourself. Like starting a new school, having to make new friends, a language you can hardly speak or read . . .

Your stomach knots up and you realize that you haven't managed to console yourself. You are still scared. In a different way.

As you worry about a billion things, you are unaware of the exact moment when the light inside your mind goes off and you are asleep. Somewhere in your dreams, a pink door opens and a black-and-white cat comes out and winks at you.

CHAPTER THREE

Plasters

W hen you wake up the next morning in your own bed, there are tears streaming down your face, even though you're unaware that you've been crying. The window next to you, streaked with rain, has been crying too. You sit up abruptly, wipe your eyes, and hold your rag doll tight. You have to get used to sleeping by yourself, that's all.

It's the school holidays, so you should go out and explore that garden you can see from your bedroom window—your garden now. Not like the workers' tenements on the island with that sad piece of grass you had to share with all the other kids. In the back corner you can see a rotary clothesline slowly spinning in a circle. When your clothes are washed, they will be hung out in private, not tethered on a long piece of bamboo from the balcony of your fifth-floor apartment so that everyone can see your old, holey underwear.

It is all yours. Even so, you look warily at the wardrobe door, now firmly shut, and you feel a strange sense of dread and confusion; a tug-of-war inside you trying to decide if you belong here or if you are a guest. Or if you're not welcome at all.

There is a sharp beep coming from outside the house, and you leap out of bed and down the stairs. You throw the front door open, and Ba Ba, down below on the driveway, is grinning out the open window of the driver's seat. Your family has its very first car. It is a tiny secondhand thing with rust patches, bald tires, and a broken taillight that has been fixed with orange cellophane. But the important thing is that it runs.

Mr. Huynh gives you a thumbs-up, and you hide behind the front door because you are in your pajamas—not the type that people buy specifically for sleeping in, with teddy bears and cartoon characters, but the clothes that you used to wear during the day, that have become so old that Ma Ma makes you wear them at night.

Ba Ba is dressed in his old work overalls that Ma Ma has cleaned up as much as possible. The overalls tell a story—with paint stains, engine grease, dried cement, and fabric burns—of all the jobs Ba Ba has ever had a go at.

They are all hard jobs, Ma Ma says, but she says you don't want to grow up and do a hard job. You want a good job where you work in a clean office as someone important, like a doctor. Everyone will look up to you and Ma Ma will be so proud. You must do well at school here so that everything, all the sacrifices and hardships your parents have made, will be worth it. Instead of lifting you up and making you feel lucky, it makes you feel leaden, as though the world is on your shoulders.

The car pulls away with another loud beep, and you lift your arm to wave but drop it down beside you with a sigh. You hide from Mrs. Huynh, who comes through the front door with a large cardboard box. You wait till she leaves before you come out from the living room.

"Come and look at this," Ma Ma says as she approaches and puts a hand on your shoulder. Ma Ma sits on a chair in the kitchen and opens the cardboard box while you sit down on the tiles. The brown-and-orange circles stare up at you curiously.

Folded at the top of the box are old baby clothes and baby bibs. Ma Ma gives them a sniff and places them lovingly on her knee. You wonder how old the

Huynhs' baby is now. Ma Ma pulls out a jacket and a pair of long pants with school logos on them that look suspiciously like they might fit you.

"Go on, try them on. This is the school you'll be going to."

You find yourself jumping off the floor as though a mouth had somehow opened in between all those brown-and-orange eyes and bitten you. Then you run away from your fears by racing out the back and loudly slamming the screen door shut. There on the back steps, you kick at the concrete all the way down.

You wonder why the house is built so high. It takes twenty-six steps to get down from the back door. From the front, you have discovered that it takes thirty steps, as the staircase bends a little. If you walk all the way down either, there is a red wooden gate on the side that should open to let you pass to the other side. But it is locked. It is arched like a hunched man with two heart-shaped holes for eyes that watch you, no matter which side you're on.

Big Scary looks down at you, surrounded by more of the tall, dark green cactus and a thin palm tree that rustles loudly like stormy weather. You search for the Room on the Roof that you could not find yesterday. It is there; it is real. From the back, though, there is no window and the eye cannot see you.

A twig cracks behind you and you turn your head. At the top of the fence, exactly where you saw that black-and-white cat, is not a pair of yellow eyes, but brown ones instead. They belong to a boy who sees that he has been caught spying, gasps, and quickly lowers himself out of sight.

Still standing on the bottom step, you look at the waist-high weeds and wonder if you are brave enough to dive straight in. There could be snakes slithering around the roots. There could be spiders and creepy-crawlies. There could be dead things. There could be anything. But then you remember that you are running from your problems and there is only one way to go and that is forward.

You jump into the grass.

You run right up to the fence and look through a hole in the wood.

Your brown eye meets another brown eye that didn't expect it, and you watch as the boy turns and flees into the Huynhs' house. Frowning, you stand up straight again, scratching your head.

The grass bends wildly in the wind, but it is only grass.

In fact, now that you stand in the middle of the wilderness of the backyard, it is actually quite boring. The little domed glasshouse looks even more rusty and broken up close. The overnight rain has streaked the panes. There are no orange trees that First Uncle died under. Maybe that was a dream. Maybe all this is one bad dream.

Curling yourself up on the bottom step, you resolve to stay out here, hoping that when the day finally goes black, you will disappear with it. But you are so hungry, your belly is aching. And you are so cold, you are shaking.

There is a little meow behind you, and you turn your head to see the black-and-white cat sitting on a step above you. Then the cat does something unusual. She lifts up one of her paws and signals you to come toward her.

You turn your head and look all the way up to the top of Big Scary and decide you've forgotten what made you upset or angry and that you need your mother's love.

So you follow the cat back up the stairs. As you decide to lift her into your arms, you find the cat is gone. All that is there is a vaguely cat-shaped rock next to the screen door, which looks as though it has been there always. Maybe First Uncle used it to prop the door open; maybe you didn't notice it before.

Or maybe the rock just winked at you.

Back inside Ma Ma takes you silently in her

arms even though you are conscious of pressing too close against her belly. There is a guest sitting at the kitchen table in the form of Mrs. Huynh with a mug of instant coffee in front of her. Like a magician, she smiles, stands up, and makes everything better.

First, she gets both Ma Ma and you to sit down. Then, from the big foam cooler she has brought over, she takes out a plastic tub of peanut cookies and places it on the table. As you stuff your mouth full of the sweet, crumbly goodness, Mrs. Huynh pulls out a bamboo steamer, and before long there is a plate of warm dumplings and red bean *baos*.

Both you and Ma Ma eat as though you haven't eaten in your whole lives (or were ready for a hearty breakfast at least). All that remains afterward is one corner of hard skin from a dumpling and the soggy paper off the bottom of the *baos*. You both stare at Mrs. Huynh as she finishes stir-frying vegetables and meat, putting them in a plastic container to cool down. There is rice cooking away in the rice cooker.

Mrs. Huynh will go, but she will come back with a cardboard box full of basic food items in cans and packets that she puts into the pantry. You watch as Ma Ma fishes out an old red packet from her bedroom and folds money into it. She tries to give it to Mrs. Huynh. Mrs. Huynh smiles in an understanding way and pushes the red packet back into Ma Ma's hands. Ma Ma's cheeks go red.

Later in the day you curl yourself into a corner of the house and daydream. Big Scary takes your body and hides it from the world. You flick through the collection of little books you have made for yourself. You write poorly in the New Language, unable to rearrange the alphabet into many correct words. You write even worse in the Old Language, the characters you attempt always sloppy, Ma Ma telling you off about your incorrect order of brushstroke. So you let pictures be your voice instead. You draw complete stories and staple them together.

You will start a new book today. And you find yourself drawing a picture of a house, with a singular room at the very top in which a giant eye that fills the entire window looks out. You draw brown-and-orange eyes. You draw heart-shaped eyes that stare out of a wooden red gate. In your corner you hide from the thought of the first day of school. You tell yourself that it's not real; you screw it up into a tiny ball and throw it into the wastepaper basket in the back of your mind.

"Are you going to buy me the toy pony?" you ask Ba Ba when he comes home from his new job at the end of a long day. But he's in no mood to talk. He doubles over with one hand on his hip, the other forming a fist to hammer on the small of his back.

"Had to carry many bags of concrete mix to the roof of the building site," he says. "I am sure they were cruel on purpose."

There is talk about asking Mr. Huynh about "unions" and "workers' rights," but you don't know what that means.

"Ma Ma says we don't have to make our own toys anymore and that I can have the pony. I want the pink one with wings and blue thunderbolts down the side."

That is when Ba Ba shouts at you.

Shocked, you take a step back.

Ba Ba puts his face in his hands and goes silent. Ma Ma swallows and puts her hand on her stomach. Silently, she takes off Ba Ba's dirty work shirt from under his undone overalls and sticks on so many capsicum plasters that his back becomes a strange, fleshy patchwork.

Ma Ma says they will suck out the aches. You will see in the morning, she says, the bottom of them will turn black, and that means they have sucked out the aches. You recoil from these giant Band-Aids; you've had one placed on yourself once and it burned. But in the morning, when they are ripped off Ba Ba, you will look—half horrified and half fascinated—at the wrinkled, shriveled skin underneath.

Right now you want to ask what you said wrong, but you don't want Ba Ba to shout at you again in case it is a question that a stupid girl would ask, and Ma Ma has explicitly told you to be a good girl. So you sit down and say nothing while Ma Ma puts a plate of rice and Mrs. Huynh's stir-fry in front of you.

You diligently eat it, even though your stomach is all clenched up and the back of your throat has that aching feeling you get when you cry. It is not until you are back up in your bedroom, a million light-years away from everyone, that you tightly hug your homemade rag doll with no name.

That night, when the wardrobe door creaks open and that slice of pink comes out, you decide you will train yourself not to run to your parents. The New Land is your home now and you cannot run from that. Even though it had always been just the three of you on the island, you never felt lonely or sad. You felt safe. You know Big Scary is trying to make you feel the same way, but it is not the same.

You hide your face under the blanket and tell yourself this feeling of fear and confusion will pass. And so too will the loneliness and sadness. You will feel better soon. You will all find your place, and everything will settle into that worn-in and comforting pocket where it was before. But everything has changed. It has changed too much to ever be good and the same again.

CHAPTER FOUR

Shoes

The house hides you from a lot of things.

The bitter cold outside.

The icy fear inside your heart.

The cool way your parents have started talking to each other.

You draw and dream and become as small as a message written on a grain of rice.

But she cannot protect you from everything.

You wake up and two weeks have flown past.

It is the first day of school.

Ma Ma is already up. She rises every day at five to make sure that Ba Ba has his morning cup of instant coffee and to pack a pot of instant noodles for his lunch.

The car also needs to be started up and the engine left to idle for fifteen minutes every morning before it can actually run. This was not mentioned by the man at the car lot who took your family's savings in cash.

Ma Ma has gone all the way down the thirty front steps to do this while Ba Ba is showering. On the way up, she trips.

"Don't tell Ba Ba," Ma Ma says.

You don't understand why. Ma Ma has always told Ba Ba everything. Looking down, you see that Ma Ma's hands are clutched together tightly. You've noticed that Ma Ma's hands tremble slightly these days as she serves dinner, as she mops the floor, and as she clutches the curtains and looks out the windows of Big Scary.

They are not the open hands that used to play mahjong with her friends on the island. The relaxed fingers that moved the softly clinking tiles adorned with Old Land characters and watching eyes.

Ma Ma goes to hide in the bedroom. You keep your promise and don't tell Ba Ba about Ma Ma tripping on the steps. He approaches you in his overalls of a million trades, and you wonder if he is going to hug you, like he used to lift you up inside his arms when you were small. Instead, he says, "Look at you, such a big girl now. Be good at school and listen to what your teacher tells you."

You think he might pat you on top of the head, but he wipes his hands on his shabby overalls instead.

"If you get an A on your first assignment, then Ba

Ba will find a way to get you that toy pony, eh? Don't look so sad."

You smile for Ba Ba and watch him descend that front staircase with his hands shoved deep into his empty pockets. At the bottom is Mrs. Huynh with more groceries, waiting eagerly to go up. Ma Ma cannot hide her relief when she sees Mrs. Huynh's face peer through the bedroom doorway. Her ankle has swollen, and Mrs. Huynh tuts as she presses a frozen bag of vegetables on it.

Mrs. Huynh keeps repeating "doctor," but Ma Ma looks scared and shakes her head. She rubs her belly uncertainly. Mrs. Huynh kneels down to your level and tries to tell you in her broken English about Dr. Vo. He is very far away, in a different suburb, but he is a good doctor. The best doctor. He can speak the same language.

Ma Ma fears doctors. She'd rather not know if she has a medical condition, preferring to think that if she pretends it doesn't exist, it will go away.

What Ma Ma fears even more about doctors is that they cost too much money.

Everything costs too much money.

It's better you walk to school by yourself without Ma Ma anyway, as you are currently burning with embarrassment. You are wearing someone's old uniform with visible worn patches on the knees and elbows. A shirt with a collar that won't sit straight; a fleece jacket that is no longer fleecy with a wonky zip. And, worst of all, boys' shoes. They are huge and grey, with black Velcro straps. It feels as though your two feet are encased in blocks of ugly concrete. You are sinking and drowning in them.

"Walk straight up to the man down the street holding the stop sign. He will let you cross the street, and from there, you will see the school. Do you understand, Meixing?"

You nod, even though it all sounds too hard. There are too many things swirling in your mind; you can't seem to concentrate on even simple instructions. But they are not simple. This is not something you have ever done before. And you have to do it alone.

You should hug Ma Ma and let her rest, but something selfish inside of you wants her to come with you, almost demands it. Because she is your mother.

Catching yourself, you are suddenly ashamed of your thoughts and, horrified, you hide them away with the other feelings you are not supposed to feel.

Ma Ma plaits your black hair into long braids on either side.

"Wait. Let me put this on. I hope it brings you good luck."

Onto your finger she slips a tiny gold ring with a Chinese character on the top. It is your grandmother's—your Ah Ma's—wedding ring. She had such tiny fingers that her wedding ring never fit any of her daughters.

"Aren't we a superstitious bunch? I hope you have a really great day, Meixing."

In the hallway the tiles the color of the earth shift so fast under your feet that you feel dizzy.

All you can see while you go down those thirty front steps of the house are your shoes. All you can see as you walk up the footpath are those shoes. You are sure that everyone is going to laugh at you. No one would want to be friends with a girl who wears boys' shoes.

Outside, there is no one around, and you worry you are too early. Or maybe you are too late and everyone is already in class. What if you are going in the wrong direction? What if today is actually still Sunday? What if it is still all a dream? Or a nightmare? But you are aware of how real everything looks.

There is always a hazy magic about Big Scary. You never see any of the mold, mildew, damp patches, or chipped paint you might expect from a house as old as her. It feels as if she is trying hard to create a fantasy for you, to keep you safe, and you move inside her as if in a dream.

Out here, though, you are exposed. Everything looks threatening. A magpie swoops so close to your head, you can feel the flap of its wings. The huge, strange trees are flesh-colored with bark that comes off in big strips. You start feeling anxious. You wish you could go back. There is a large crack in the pavement in front of you.

As instructed, you march right up to the man dressed in a white coat holding a stop sign. You are too shy to look at him, so you give him a side glance and step onto the zebra crossing.

What happens next is a loud scream and a car stopping inches from your body. You feel yourself being pulled back by your collar and you stare at the Lollipop Man, who you know is angry, he's just too shocked to shout at you.

He thinks you're a silly girl who doesn't even know how to cross the road. And he's right. You are a silly girl who doesn't know how to cross the road. Back where you came from, there were hardly any cars. Or roads, for that matter. The workers' housing buildings, the deep wounds in the ground from where the machines took out that precious Earth Dust, and the handful of shops were the only blights on the island. Beyond that was jungle and dirt tracks, and you went wherever you wanted. You were wild and free, and you climbed trees and lounged in them like a monkey.

The Lollipop Man holds up his flags to stop the traffic, and he looks over to you. It is your signal to cross, but you are too scared to move. What if you walk too fast? What if you walk too slow? Now he thinks you're even more stupid. You tremble violently.

So you stand there unable to do anything until a mother and two children come along, and you disappear into them and pass over to the other side pretending you are part of them. You wish as hard as you can that your shoes change into pink-and-white ones like the girl is wearing.

Standing by a utility pole is the boy from the Huynhs' residence. He has the angriest look on his face; fists clenched. You let the mother with the two kids pass and you stand there, staring at him.

The boy from next door is ripping the yellow flyers that were pasted on the pole, scrunching them up and throwing them on the ground, stomping on them with a foot. When he realizes that someone is watching him, he turns around. He is one head taller than you. He stares at you so long that you feel you might burst into flames from the embarrassment. He is looking at your school uniform and your shoes. It suddenly occurs to you that his mother has given you his hand-me-downs. You want the ground to open up and for you to be slowly lowered down; for the grass to cover your head so it is as if you were never there.

He opens his mouth to say something, but then he closes it again. He takes off. You can feel your face burning bright red. Slowly, you walk up to where he was standing and look down at the crushed paper. You can't read the writing, but you look at the ugly face that the boy has ripped in half. It is a strange drawing of a man with a triangle hat, a thin mustache, and slits for eyes, with a big red cross mark over him.

Miss Cicely, your new primary school teacher, is enthusiastic to introduce you to her classroom and students. It feels as though you can't move your jaw to talk, you are still so anxious. The Huynh boy is sitting in the back, and he sinks lower into his chair when he sees you, his long legs pressing under the bottom of his desk. You are introduced to a girl with blond pigtails that your teacher talks to fondly, and you sit down next to her.

She makes it obvious from her expression what she thinks of your secondhand clothes and boys' shoes. You desperately wish for the checked school dress she is wearing under her sweater and the neat white sneakers with the pale purple shoelaces on her feet. She looks with distaste at the burlap bag that you are carrying your school things in. At the plastic ziplock bag you place on the desk that contains a few basic stationery items.

Her eyes light up when she sees the little gold ring on your middle finger.

"We can be friends," she says with quiet deliberation.

You swallow nervously and say nothing. You twist the ring round and round your finger.

The class is given an activity where you have to insert the correct words into the correct sentences. *Elaborate. Exaggerate. Unanimous.* You can hardly read what is in front of you.

"You can copy my work," your new friend whispers, but you shake your head, as Ma Ma has always taught you to be humble and honest. So you guess the answers and hope for the best.

"Do you mind if I borrow your eraser?" asks Miss Cicely, smiling down at you.

The correct answer is no.

As in, *No. I don't mind.*

But the New Language confuses you, and because you would love Miss Cicely to borrow your eraser, you say yes.

And it is the wrong answer.

"You can borrow mine if you like, Miss Cicely," your friend pipes up, and the teacher takes her eraser.

You stare mournfully down at the floor because you realize you've made a mistake, but you don't know what to do about it now. You catch a glimpse of those boys' shoes on your feet and your eyes shoot back up. You promise yourself you will try harder to be smarter next time.

Miss Cicely hands out the worksheets from before winter break, which she has now finished marking. From behind you, there is a loud commotion, and you turn around in time to see the Huynh boy stand up and rip the paper handed to him into little pieces.

"How many times have I told you this is unacceptable behavior? To the principal's office, again!" Miss Cicely sighs and puts her face in her hands.

The Huynh boy gets up and runs out of the classroom, slamming the door behind him.

"He's angry with himself because he is stupid," your new friend explains. "He always gets all the answers wrong."

Your heart does a flip-flop and you wish like crazy that you'll get at least some of the answers right today. In your head you imagine you get everything correct. In your head your teacher becomes very fond of you, and she tells Ma Ma what a great student you are. In your head the girl sitting next to you loves you too and becomes your best friend. Everything is going to turn out fine. But if it is, why do you have to wish so desperately for it?

CHAPTER FIVE

Ring

M a Ma says that you will enjoy learning at the new school as much as you did at the old school. And it's true, you loved that tiny class where the teacher treated you like a daughter and it was like going over to a friend's place every day. Sometimes it felt as though you were playing more than you were studying. You had learned both the Old and the New Language at the same time, but neither well. It was the best the little school could offer, on a little island that did not have much at all.

Here, though, you have to sit up straight and pay attention to everything. This is serious; your grades must be good, you mustn't mess up. Your parents are depending on it. You will get good grades and that will get you the toy pony. You know that you should enjoy school and learning, but you sit in your seat hoping for it to end. You can't help but feel relieved when it is finally time for lunch.

All the students eat outside in the covered assembly area. The wind howls from one open end to the other and threatens to lift the roof off. Even though it looks like a chaos of bodies and lunch boxes and echoing voices, there appears to be some sort of order. Groups of students have claimed the painted outlines of hopscotch and handball as their special areas. Other groups sit on the plain concrete. Then there are the students who sit by themselves on the very edges. The Huynh boy is one of them.

With a terrible feeling in your stomach, you realize that you are also one of them and you will have to sit on the edge too. Until your new friend comes up and invites you to join a group from your class. They sit inside a magic purple circle that you imagine is used for some secret game that you'll learn to play one day. You are both relieved and more shaken than ever.

Your metal tiffin box—your lunch tin—sits on your lap. You don't want to open it because you know it's not going to contain anything like the white-bread sandwiches the other girls are eating, filled with a thin slice of something yellow and something pink. From the corner of your eye, across the assembly area, you see the Huynh boy taking out a chicken wing and attacking it hungrily. Not caring what anyone thinks of him. Your stomach gurgles, and not out of hunger.

You take a sharp breath and flick the lunch box open.

The girls suddenly stop their conversations.

"Eww, are you going to eat *that* with your *fingers*?"

"Eww, it's got bones. I can't eat chicken with bones. I only like chicken nuggets."

The girls take dainty bites out of their sandwiches, and you can't bring yourself to eat your lunch with those curious eyes on you. Even though you love chicken wings and you eat them all the time. *With your fingers.*

After they have finished their sandwiches and you have sat there hungrily after closing your lunch box and staring quietly, the girls decide to have cartwheel and handstand competitions. They ask you to join, but you decline because you can't do either. Other kids come and watch and admire, and you find yourself jammed shoulder to shoulder with these onlookers. You blend into the crowd and then find yourself pushed back. Your shoulders slack and sag. It is obvious that you do not fit in with this group of girls.

Fearing that there will be more things involving

reading and writing after lunch, you are glad when you find out that the class is going to do art. You walk to a special wing of the school that houses little art rooms, and there today, with Miss Hornbuckle, you are making flags for an upcoming special celebration.

Your new friend insists on sitting next to you, even though she should have realized what a disaster you are and lost interest by now.

Oh, dear. You have no idea what the flag looks like. You are secretly relieved when your art teacher draws one on the board for everyone. You copy the design and the colors.

Painting is messy work. But it is messy work that you love, and for the first time all day you feel at peace with yourself. Everything will work itself out, and before you know it, you will be grown up and not have to worry anymore. It is hard to grip the paintbrush properly wearing Ah Ma's gold ring, so you take it off and place it on the corner of the desk, just beyond the paper.

From the adjoining desk, your friend looks keenly at the shiny band. It only takes a second for you to turn away and stir your paintbrush in the jar of dirty water. When your eyes go back to the corner of the desk, Ah Ma's ring is gone.

You are certain that there is a little weight inside the front pocket of your friend's painting smock of the same corresponding size. But overwhelmed by the thought that someone would do something like that, and by the realization that your new friend is nothing but a nasty thief, you do something unexpected.

You burst into tears. The whole class looks at you while ugly, fat tears roll down your cheeks and your mouth makes a terrible wailing noise.

Miss Hornbuckle tries to work out what is wrong, but the words you know of the language are useless in beginning to explain to her. You are crying too hard anyway.

Your art teacher puts it down to it being the first day of school and that it has been a long journey for this new girl to get to this New Land. She thinks the best thing for you would be to sit on the bench outside the classroom and catch some fresh air.

It really is the worst thing she could have done. Sitting by yourself outside, you feel frighteningly abandoned, as though you are being punished somehow. It is this thought that breaks your heart a little and stops you from crying any further. You wipe your face down with the back of your hands.

The next thing you realize is that the Huynh boy is unexpectedly sitting next to you. When you turn, all you can see is the crisp and clear logo on his new uniform. The old jacket of his that you're wearing has been washed so many times that the logo has cracked and taken on the appearance of an evil skull.

"Can you understand the language everyone speaks in this country?" he asks in a snarl.

You nod.

"Look, I saw Paige take your ring and put it into her front pocket. Do you want me to tell the teacher?"

You stare at him.

"Can you speak?"

Of course you can. What type of dumb question is that? In fact, you have so much you want to say, so many emotions brimming inside of you, so many stories of things you've seen and experienced, waiting to come out . . .

Just not today. Not right now.

"There you are! Did I say you could leave your desk, Kevin?"

Kevin Huynh looks down at his feet. "No, Miss Hornbuckle," he mumbles.

"Then please come back inside."

"Yes, Miss Hornbuckle."

"What do you have to say first?"

"Sorry, Miss Hornbuckle."

The art teacher shakes her head and folds her arms, striding back inside.

Kevin turns to you and says, "They probably wouldn't believe me anyway," before his hunched frame disappears from sight.

It was really nice of Kevin to want to help, but you are still confused by him. All your life you've been told to do everything your parents and teachers tell you to do. You don't know why he behaves the way he does. Why doesn't Mrs. Huynh just tell him to be a good boy? Ma Ma tells you to be a good girl. Suddenly, you find yourself thinking about this not with love and respect, as you've always been taught, but with a bitter resentfulness.

When you get back to class with Miss Cicely, you confront your supposed new friend yourself by pointing at her.

"I can't understand you," she replies with a sweet smile. That is all she has to say to you because you both know what she means.

When it's dismissal time, now that you know how the school crossing works, you wait for a group of kids to reach the edge of the walkway and then you hide among them. You are still too embarrassed to face the Lollipop Man alone. As soon as you get to the other side of the street, you are running, tearing out the bands of your braids. The too-big shoes slap the pavement loudly, your heart thumping in your ears. At the top of the thirty steps you kick the cursed things off your feet and you run straight into the safety of Big Scary.

You can hear Ma Ma moving somewhere inside, but the house is so big, you cannot tell where. You freeze in the hallway, wipe down your face with a hand, and listen. It is the clang of a mop bucket being pushed around. You are trying to work out if Ma Ma is upstairs or downstairs when something small and shiny falls past your eye. It hits the tiles with a ping and spins furiously.

When it comes to a stop, you kneel down and pick it up. It is a small silver disk with a hole punched in the center. You look up, and Big Scary taps you a pink message along the wall, as if to say, *What do you think?*

You feel compelled to thread your finger through the disk to see if it fits, but before it is even on, you rip it off again. It is not the same. Nothing is the same. You place it on the side table for Ba Ba to find and put back into the house wherever it came from, and you run away down the hall. Big Scary seems to sag all around you in disappointment.

CHAPTER SIX

Chicken

꙰

Ba Ba is home early, arriving not long after you do, and he says he is going to take you out to eat, as a family. You don't know where the money has come from because there is supposed to be no money. Even Ma Ma is giving him that look, but it is a nice idea, so you head down to the car. Ba Ba holds Ma Ma's hand tightly as they descend the steps; you watch this and it makes you feel safe and secure. Inside this moment, everything is good.

The little junk heap of a car putts along with the three of you in it, occasionally backfiring.

"This car is worse than the dune buggy we had back on the island," says Ma Ma.

"Don't lie, you loved that dune buggy," replies Ba Ba.

Ma Ma leans her elbow against the window, and

when she turns her head, you can see a smile on her face.

"You used to tear along the beach in that buggy real fast," says Ba Ba. "For someone who doesn't have a driver's license."

"Shush," says Ma Ma. She is still smiling.

It starts to drizzle. As the windshield wipers scrape ineffectively at the rain, you nervously rub at the skin where the gold ring should be. You feel you can't tell your mother the truth. You can't admit that you were foolish enough to take it off. You can't admit that she trusted you with such a precious treasure and you broke that trust. Most of all, you can't face the fact that the ring was supposed to bring you luck and all it has given you is misery.

You are fearful that Ma Ma is going to ask for it back before bedtime, and your fingers clench tightly. You sit in the backseat stiffly and don't make a sound, even though, inside your head, another version of you is pressed up against the window, looking at the tracks of the rain and humming a happy tune.

It isn't a proper restaurant, it is only the fried chicken chain at a run-down shopping center, but you have seen the ads for it on TV so you are excited. You approach the counter, a little shy, and the girl behind the counter smiles at you. Ma Ma, though, is less enthused. She takes one look at the menu above the counter, her face goes red, and she says that the prices are ridiculous and that you are leaving right now.

Ba Ba tells her to stay, to order something small. Ma Ma looks at him like he is mad and calmly says that she would like to instead buy her daughter a new school uniform or pay back Mrs. Huynh for the groceries she has brought over and hasn't accepted any payment for. She does not want "something small."

Ma Ma goes to leave, but Ba Ba refuses to go, and the next thing you know, Ma Ma and Ba Ba are having an argument inside the store. You stare in disbelief, and it's as though the cheerful radio music playing has suddenly been shut off and inside your head is a piercing drone.

The girl behind the counter is embarrassed and angles her body as if to go, but she must be forced to stay when there are customers. Your mind searches for that black-and-white cat to lead you away. Her face comes into view, sniffs curiously, and then pulls back. She cannot help you here.

Eventually, Ma Ma storms off.

You want to tell her that being upset might make the baby decide to arrive on the spot, but Ma Ma is standing in the parking lot with her back to you and her hands over her ears. The drive home is silent and upsetting. You discover you have nervously rubbed the skin around your middle finger red.

Once home, you expect everything to be safe and okay again, but it is the beginning of something worse. In the hallway Ba Ba admits that he quit his job this morning.

"So you decided that the smart thing would be to take us somewhere to spend the little money we have left?" Ma Ma is shouting angrily.

"I wanted to do something nice for the family!"

"You wanted to soften me up! You wanted to be the good guy in front of Meixing!"

You shrink against the wooden paneling, and it suddenly feels as though either the wall is too tall or you have become too small. You press against Big Scary, and the house curves herself to shelter you.

"I can't keep doing it anymore. They make me do all the worst tasks and the heaviest lifting. It's killing me, Ping."

Ma Ma pauses to rub her tummy.

"Why don't we sell this house? We can buy something smaller and have some money left over," says Ba Ba.

"We are not selling the house!" Ma Ma yells, and

then painfully restrains herself. "This house belonged to my brother."

"So he finds it fit to leave us a house in his will, but no money to run the thing? Do you know how much electricity, heating, and cooling cost to run a house this size?"

You hope Big Scary cannot hear your parents talk about her in such an impersonal way. You find yourself sucking your thumb like you did when you were a baby, and you toss your hand aside, disgusted.

"My brother left all his money to the local cat shelter because he is a good person, okay? Do you know how selfish you sound? He wanted us to live in this house as a family. If it wasn't for his invitation, we wouldn't be here!"

"Life was better before," Ba Ba says quietly.

He is defeated, but Ma Ma does not look like a winner.

"Sometimes I wonder why we ever came here," says Ba Ba.

You know why they came here. They came for *you*. To give you a better life, to give you a better education. You'd rather you not exist and you close your eyes. You can feel a second heartbeat along with your own and you know it is Big Scary saying that she is with you and not to give up. You touch the dark brown wood, and underneath, your fingers glow a neon pink.

"Let's not fight about it anymore," says Ma Ma in a whisper. "I will talk to Mrs. Huynh next door. They run a little bakery in the city. Maybe they will feel sorry for us and can get you a job there."

"I don't want anyone to feel sorry for us," replies Ba Ba.

"Chun! Don't turn your back on me!" pleads Ma Ma. "I'll sell my grandmother's ring if I have to. Can we please talk?"

Ah Ma's ring, you think with a stab in your heart. You nervously hold your finger.

Ba Ba leaves. The front door slams, and the amber panel violently shakes but holds in place. The argument is closed. Ba Ba on one side and Ma Ma on the other.

You hear the car start and you listen to its engine, trying to follow what turns and which streets it might be taking, until all you can hear is the silence of the rain.

Ah Ma's ring, you say to yourself again.

"Ma Ma?"

You find her sitting in the kitchen with her face in her hands, and she is gently weeping. You take the box of tissues out of the pantry and place it quietly in front of her. You lay your face for a moment across her shoulders and you try not to let a sigh accidentally escape, try not to touch her too much.

"You're a good girl, Meixing," she says in a breath between sobs. She puts a hand on your arm. "I learned a new local word today. 'Amazing.' Amazing Meixing!"

She tries to laugh. You think she is wrong, though. You are not amazing. You are a disappointment, a burden, and a coward. It feels as though it's only a matter of time before everyone realizes these things. That your parents made that trip all the way here in the hope that you would be something special; but you are just not worth the effort.

There is a soft knock at the front door and you find Mrs. Huynh standing there with food-filled containers, balanced on top of one another. She seems to have an endless supply of plastic boxes, even though the ones she brought yesterday are still sitting in the sink, unwashed.

Ma Ma cannot speak her language and, in turn, Mrs. Huynh cannot speak yours. But they have become friends through gestures and smiles and bump gazing. Mrs. Huynh has learned that your parents don't eat beef and are wary of her spices and sauces, so she has pared her cooking down to that point where both cultures agree to meet. Shredded chicken and noodles in broth. Stir-fried vegetables and tofu. Spring rolls, as everyone, anywhere, loves spring rolls.

Mrs. Huynh sees a hot, crying Ma Ma, and the first thing she does is put a gentle hand on her back. You see the loving expression on Mrs. Huynh's face, the deep lines that appear around her eyes, her forehead, her lips, and you think she is so kind. At the same time you cannot help but feel jealous that Mrs. Huynh is allowed to get so close to Ma Ma when you have to be so careful with her all the time. You thought you were her Amazing Meixing.

Looking down at your scrawny body and your shaking hands, you back off. Mrs. Huynh opens the pantry and takes down the tin of cocoa powder.

Out in the backyard, with the long grass flattened over your scrunched-down body like a green cocoon, you worry for everyone. You worry that your father is being bullied. You worry that your mother is finding it hard to cope. You worry that when your baby brother or sister is born, they will not know the happiness that you had known when you lived on your island.

Big Scary has nothing to say to you. She has

gone dark and it's possible that she's fallen asleep. Maybe she can't help you when you're out here. But you don't want to go back inside because you want to be free.

A scraping sound comes from the fence and you think maybe Kevin is back again. It turns out to be the black-and-white cat, looking very formal in her tuxedo, having a second think about the long grass.

To show her that it isn't scary at all, you gently lift her off the fence and down onto the path that you have flattened from the back steps to the middle of the garden. The cat winks at you, jumps out of your arms, and is gone—through a broken pane in the glasshouse.

That's when you make the decision to follow her. *Be brave,* you tell yourself as you twist the handle of the door. It opens, you step inside, and your world changes.

CHAPTER SEVEN

Oranges

The glasshouse is a broken-down thing on the outside. Smashed and rusted, the remaining glass panels are milky and opaque. One entire wall is missing and has been mended with mismatched doors and windows. But like people, sometimes things aren't the same on the inside as they are on the outside.

The first thing you think is that it is much bigger in here than you thought it would be.

The second thing is that you finally understand where First Uncle kept all his orange trees.

Spread out before you is an entire orchard. You stare in surprise at what is in front of you. You look behind you, and it appears that what is inside cannot be contained, as the whole backyard is now filled with orange trees. You leave the door open.

A pink serpent, looking for all the world like it

escaped from the neon glow of Big Scary's wardrobe, hisses at you as you approach. You take a step back and it disappears into the branches of a tree. You aren't scared because the sun is spreading reassuring rays over to you from the east. This is a sun you can stare straight at, and she has a beautiful face.

Above, beyond the ornate arches and through the glass roof, it feels as if you can see on and on until forever. Higher up, the full moon with a hint of a smile on her full red lips is sleeping in the sky. You want to know why the sun and the moon appear at the same time, but you don't think there is anyone around to answer your question.

Until you see the shape of a person in the distance, all the way in the back of the glasshouse. You run toward the shape, and although it feels as if you're covering an awfully long distance, at the same time it feels as if you're running on the spot.

You reach out your hand and close your eyes, and you compel your mind to take you where you want to go and need to be. Everything goes silent. The voice of your mother shouting. The voice of your father shouting back. The voice of you, scolding yourself. It all goes quiet, and you are floating around in the space where your stories and your drawings come to life. That special place that is yours and yours alone, where nothing is denied and everything is possible. You feel yourself propel forward and away you go, free.

You are puffing when you reach him.

"Hello, Meixing. I wondered how long it would take you to get here."

"I thought you were supposed to be dead, First Uncle," you reply.

So you can talk, despite what Kevin or anyone at school or even your parents think. You can talk when you have a chance to breathe.

"That I am," he says with a chuckle. "It happened so suddenly, I almost didn't even realize. I would say it was the thing I feared the most when I was alive. Now I realize it just means I have more time to do gardening."

"I also thought I was supposed to be scared of you, now that you're a ghost," you say.

"Maybe you are confusing ghosts with the cruel people of this world," Uncle says.

The air is filled with the scent of sweet, pale blossoms. First Uncle has been picking oranges and piling them into his wheelbarrow, and he shows you the one he has in his hand. It is the most orange-colored orange you have ever seen, with dark, waxy leaves. The pink serpent slithers past his shoulder, but Uncle doesn't seem scared of it.

"I have very fond memories of oranges," explains First Uncle. "When I was young, they used to be a rare and special treat for Chinese New Year and other occasions. Would you like to plant something yourself?"

On the gardening table you find a wooden case separated into little compartments, which—to your surprise when you lift the lid—contains every single seed in the world. But only one of each. There are some enormous pods that you believe will grow into giants, but you pass your hands over them and select a tiny black seed, no bigger than a speck of dirt really. First Uncle squats with you while you poke a hole in the ground, drop it in, and spread the dirt back on top.

"Why isn't anything happening?" you ask as you stare at the ground.

"You haven't watered it," says First Uncle, passing you a metal can.

"Oh. I see."

The single drop of water reflects the world, but upside down, falling in slow motion and shattering into a million pieces as it hits the soil. The plant inside the seed unfurls within itself. It becomes a million things all at the same time, because here, under the glasshouse of infinite possibilities, it can. From that one seed, a million seedlings grow and a sea of green rushes outward from you.

As the seedlings grow and form new leaves and shudder under the atmosphere, you see your entire life grow from when you were a baby. You were born a long way from the home of your parents on a little island. Ma Ma and Ba Ba came there with the other families when they opened up the ground with machinery, to help take out the precious Earth Dust or, like Ba Ba, to help scratch out a little settlement from the jungle. Ba Ba was not good at painting (he's color-blind) and not very good at woodwork (every-thing he made was wonky), but he was pretty good at driving around a concrete truck, so that's what he did most.

You used to watch the bright red crabs migrate every spring from the jungle down to the ocean, and you would stand on the edge of the water and squint, hoping you could see the New Land. Ma Ma told you that she and Ba Ba were too old to make the very most of what the New Land would provide, but one day it would all be for you. They were the guardians. You were the hope.

The seedlings mature into plants and they bud and flower. As far as your eye can see are blue forget-me-nots. You kneel down among the paper-thin petals and you feel your heart become unbearably sad. The sky is blue. The ground below you is blue. Everything is blue, including you.

"Meixing? Meixing, where have you gone?"

At first you think it is First Uncle talking to you, but then you realize it's Ma Ma's voice, coming from a very faraway place that you don't know if you can return to. Or if you want to.

But the voice keeps calling, more urgent and plaintive this time, and you realize you must try. You get up and you run, stirring up the forget-me-not petals so that they swirl around you like blue confetti and threaten to stick to you and stain you forever. You bolt through the orange orchard, running for the open door. The pink serpent hisses at you.

"Uncle, why are there no stars in the sky?" you shout, the question suddenly occurring to you. But it is too late, you have tumbled out; the door closes and everything is ordinary again.

CHAPTER EIGHT

Blues

You bend over to pick a leaf up off the ground; it is still fresh, dark green and waxy. You look around, but the world and all its orange trees have disappeared.

It's getting dark outside, and you wonder how long you've been gone. It could have been minutes; it could have been years. The frantic sound of your mother's voice makes you abandon your thoughts and race up the back steps. The black-and-white cat jumps hastily out of the way.

"Where have you been?" Ma Ma exclaims, standing there looking entirely lost within herself. "I thought you'd gone missing too! Ba Ba hasn't come back."

Ma Ma sits down at the kitchen table with her face in her hands. She starts sobbing, and Mrs. Huynh puts a reassuring palm on her shoulder. You've never felt so useless in your life.

"Maybe he's gone to buy me that toy pony."

Those are the words that escape from your mouth, and you realize too late that you are only thinking of yourself when you should be thinking about Ma Ma. You should be speaking the right words of comfort. You should be that filial daughter in your Old Language learner books. Ma Ma cries even harder. But that blue inside you wants her to acknowledge that this is your pain too.

Ba Ba will be back soon, you reassure yourself. He will cool down and realize that an argument over fried chicken and money is not worth staying out in the cold and the rain, and that he should come home, where it's warm and where his family is. At the very least, he'll get hungry and he'll be back for dinner. Mrs. Huynh has brought over her own chicken dish, and it's probably better than the one at the shop anyway.

Dinner comes and goes. Ba Ba is still not home. It is dark now. Ma Ma is still sitting where she was hours ago. Mrs. Huynh is still here. You start wondering about adult things like should she go home and have dinner with her own family, because Ma Ma is currently not available to think these thoughts. She sits there opposite you like a statue with only the eyes moving, blinking every so often. The frown on her face is fixed.

Presently, there is a call from the front door, and you all turn expectantly, hearts lifting in hope, but it is the voice of Mr. Huynh. Mrs. Huynh goes to let him in, and he pops his head through the kitchen archway. Unexpectedly, so does Kevin.

You stare at Kevin. He is wearing some sort of fluffy robe with a superhero on it riding a large green cat, belted around the waist. You think he might be wearing pajamas underneath. Kevin sees you staring at him, and he goes red and kicks at the baseboards. Mrs. Huynh reprimands him, and he scowls and mutters things under his breath that could be swear words, until Mrs. Huynh twists his ear for it.

There is some discussion among the Huynhs in a language that is not yours and not the New Language, either, and Mrs. Huynh sends them off. You expect that she will send you to bed too, since it is late, but she lets you stay at the kitchen table and do some drawing.

It feels forbidden that you should be doing anything but staring at the clock on the wall and worrying alongside Ma Ma. As you start making a tiny new stapled-together book of drawings, you feel guilty about acting so normal. You can hear every single scratch the lead pencil makes on the paper and it etches itself into your heart.

You stare long and hard at the blue coloring pencil. Seizing and gripping it as if you had to hold on for dear life, you draw an endless field of blue flowers and an endless blue sky and a girl who is completely blue. You collapse all of this into the little pages you have cut from one piece of white paper. The wall behind you creaks and moans, and you put a hand behind you and touch Big Scary. You feel a warmth against your palm and turn to see the pink glow that just as soon disappears when you pull away. You look at the adults, but they don't seem to notice.

It is getting much later than anyone, even someone trying to shake off an argument, would stay out. Mrs. Huynh rings home in case Ba Ba is there, but you all know that he isn't. She doesn't ring anyone after that because there isn't anyone else to ring. Eventually, she has to go back to her own family even though she is torn about leaving you and Ma Ma. What a fragile, useless lot you both are.

Then, midnight. And you are still wide awake. And Ba Ba is still not home.

Ma Ma has fallen asleep with her arms folded on the kitchen table. For a moment you think you must have become invisible, as you haven't been told to go to bed and it's been hours since your mother has even acknowledged you.

The picture book is finished, and for some reason you feel you need to hide it, so into the ziplock bag you use as a pencil case it goes. Back into the burlap bag you carry in place of a backpack.

There is a knock on the door, very soft. You look at Ma Ma. She is fast asleep, a bit of drool dripping out of her open mouth and onto the kitchen table. The knock comes again and you reassure yourself that it's Ba Ba come home.

In your heart you know it's not. He would just let himself in.

It's okay to open the front door, you tell yourself, because there is a locked screen door between you and any stranger you should find on the other side. The sandy tiles underneath your feet shift faster than ever.

Standing on the front step are two police officers, and the first thing you think is that you are going to jail. You're not sure why. Your parents have said that you are all welcome to come to this New Land, and First Uncle had said before he died that you were all welcome to stay at his house. After he died, he even gave you the house. Yet you're still scared you've done something wrong.

Maybe there has been a mistake. Maybe someone has changed their mind—First Uncle is still alive and he doesn't want in his house people who are so unhappy about being there; or the New Land has decided you are not good enough to be here. You cannot speak the language, you don't have any money, you don't fit in, you need to go back to where you came from for everyone's sake.

On the inside you know that you wouldn't be able to hide your relief if it was all a mistake, if you were all sent packing back to your island.

"Is there an adult we can talk to?" the policewoman says gently, but your fears switch to the fact that you might be in trouble because you're still awake on a school night. Why has your mother let you stay up so late? She must be a bad mother. Maybe they will take her away and lock her up. You turn hot and cold and hot again.

"Hello?" says the tired voice of Ma Ma behind you, but it doesn't make it any better. In fact, it's much worse when the four of you are around the kitchen table. Three hot mugs of instant coffee sit untouched. Ma Ma has her arm around you and it makes you feel a little safer. But at the same time it also breaks your heart because she is leaning on you. She knows less of the New Language than you do, and she needs you to tell her what the police have to say. It is too much of a burden to bear.

"Can you please tell your mother that there has been an accident."

You are so relieved that you understand this sentence that you quickly translate it to Ma Ma without taking in what it means. Ma Ma goes stiff and pale. You feel her dread spreading from her to yourself; the icy touch of her hand passes straight through your skin and freezes you deeply on the inside, as if you'll never be warm again.

"I'm afraid that your father was involved in a car accident."

"I'm sorry, but it was fatal."

You don't need to translate anything to Ma Ma for her to start crying. She cradles her stomach and looks down. Cries. You start crying too. The police eventually leave, but the crying goes on. You try to reach out for Ma Ma, but she doesn't see you; she goes straight to her room and closes the door. She is shutting herself in. But she is also shutting you out.

So you go to your room too, but it feels as though you are floating off to another universe. You are upstairs and in your bed, and there is crying coming from you and crying rising up from the bottom floor. For a moment you become so light-headed that you forget what you are crying for, just that you can't stop.

In the absence of something warm and human you try holding on to your rag doll, but the scratchy and ugly thing reminds you of how poor your old life was and how you are not supposed to be poor anymore. You put her away under the bed, but that leaves you with nothing.

You think about Ba Ba and how he wanted to order you the fried chicken like the one on TV and how Ma Ma got angry and made you all leave. You stop crying and lie down on your pillow, exhausted.

A warmth appears on your shoulder that is touching the wall. You don't turn around to acknowledge it. In fact, you shift forward on the bed away from the wall. Big Scary opens your closet door, and that neon pink glow comes out.

Getting up out of bed, you slam the door shut. It stays shut. You feel the house cower in surprise and shrink a little. The bedroom door becomes closer; your bed takes up more space. But you don't care.

All of a sudden your head is filled with Ma Ma's voice, nagging you to change into your pajamas. What if you refuse? If she were a good mother, she would not have started that argument in the chicken shop; she should have sacrificed herself for you and put on a happy smile. If she were a good mother, you wouldn't be wearing old rags to bed, you'd be wearing a fluffy robe like Kevin's, except it would be pink and have a girl cartoon on it. A princess of power raising her glittering magic sword high into the air.

As suddenly as it comes, the voice goes. You search your heart and remember that Ma Ma only stormed out of the chicken place because she said she'd rather buy you new clothes than have a chicken meal for herself. You know if Ma Ma had money, you would have a pink fluffy robe. This makes you start weeping, and you hold on to the thought until it fades and contracts into a tiny pinpoint of light inside your head.

Drifting in and out of sleep that night, every time you find yourself awake, you hear crying. Sometimes it is coming from you; other times you are aware of being silent, but the crying is still there.

You don't want to face the wall, but you are forced to turn over when one whole side of your body becomes numb. You try to keep your eyes shut and to not look at Big Scary. But you awake at one point to find she has drawn you a picture in pink light. It is a crude, lopsided heart.

CHAPTER NINE

Rolls

W hen you wake the next day and go down the stairs, Ma Ma is not up and about like the days before. It is completely silent. There is no sound of the car down below, backfiring away before it decides it can finally go; there is no bustling in the kitchen and no cheap instant coffee. All the birds that sing in the morning, the magpies and the mudlarks of the world, might as well be dead.

You peep in the bedroom, and the first thing that hits you is that Ba Ba is not there on his side of the bed. And for a moment of alarm you think Ma Ma is gone too, but she's under the covers and not moving.

In your panic you shake her a little too hard, and a hand comes out and then a sharp voice asking you to leave her alone. You keep patting her through the sheet because you want her to say that she's still there, and there for you. Angrily, Ma Ma tosses the blanket aside and stands up on Big Scary's shaggy fur.

Ma Ma's face is red, her eyes almost glued shut, and you reel from this monster you don't recognize. You turn to run away, and it is only that familiar voice commanding you to stop that makes you do so. She says you need to get ready for school and to be a big girl today and do it without her help.

You want to stay home with her. She tells you not to disobey her and that you are going to school, realizing too late how loudly she is shouting at you before she bursts into tears. You flee from your parents' room. Except it is no longer your parents' room. Your mother stays and cries.

In the fridge you find a small polystyrene tray with a sticky label that reads HUYNH'S HAPPY BAKERY. You recognize what is inside as spring rolls, but instead of being brown from deep-frying, they are white and translucent; you can see straight through them to the beautiful rainbow-colored vegetables inside. As you unwrap the plastic and arrange them on a plate for your breakfast, you wonder if you have permission to grieve today or if you have to keep it all inside. Tears flow so fast, they hit the rainbow rolls, and you are in such a hurry to wipe them away from your face that you answer your own question. You convince yourself it's because you don't want a damp breakfast. The spring rolls taste fresh and delicious—as good as rainbows—and they cheer you up a little on the inside. You finish the whole lot off and go back upstairs to get dressed.

It is easier to wear those ugly boys' shoes the second time.

It is also easier to cross the street as you hide behind a bush and wait for a crowd to walk with. So far it feels that all you have learned in this New Land is how to be invisible and how to lose yourself. It is so cold outside. But it is nothing compared to how cold it is inside yourself.

The girl who used to be your friend is already in the classroom. Only when you get close enough do you realize that she is wearing your grandmother's ring. The girl stole the ring from you, made you cry, and now she is showing up to school wearing it like a trophy.

She watches you watching her hand, and she says, "Do you like it? My mother bought it for me."

You want to say something, you really do, but then you realize that it is not worth the fight. What does it matter anymore? Your father is gone. You don't have the energy to find the right words and then put them in the right order.

She's no longer interested in being your friend because she has from you what she wanted. She turns away, giving you the cold shoulder. You are once again left rubbing the empty flesh around your middle finger. You know that from this point forward, you are no longer welcome to sit with her in class or join her group for lunch.

Miss Cicely decides to start the day with show-and-tell. The girl who used to be your friend puts her hand excitedly in the air and marches confidently to the front of the room. She explains that she's a model now and holds up the catalogue of a local gardening center where she poses with her family, pretending to buy potted plants.

Your teacher asks you to go next, and you bring out the little stapled-together picture book from your ziplock bag. Page by page you show the class the pictures inside—Big Scary viewed from the front, the giant eye in the mystery Room on the Roof, the neon pink lights at the bottom of the wardrobe, the pink serpent and the glasshouse in the backyard where you planted a seed and turned everything blue.

You think of the name of the activity itself—show-and-tell—and you wish you could tell everyone the shock, the pain, and the unbelievability of your father being gone. Momentarily, you stall and hang your head. The class mistakes this for shyness.

You continue and show them the second-to-last page, where you have drawn First Uncle, smiling and waving among his orange orchard. Then the last page, a girl turned completely blue.

Miss Cicely watches and doesn't say a word. Maybe she thought that you were some amazing person—the Amazing Meixing of Ma Ma's dreams—from a faraway place who had exotic tales of culture and wonder to tell. Instead, all you can offer are your weird drawings. You can't even open your mouth to say hi, let alone anything remotely exotic or wonderful. You are not amazing. You sit back down.

The results from yesterday's activity are handed back out, and out of a possible fifteen check marks, you have scored fifteen red crosses. You are mortified. Your guessing is so bad that you couldn't even get one answer right by chance. You think of your mother and feel a little sick. She's going to think you are dumb, useless, not their great hope. Not even close to being close. Ba Ba will hit you with the bamboo handle of the chicken feather duster, you think automatically. Then in an instant the realization jams itself up into a lump of sorrow in your throat.

You would happily hold out your hand and feel the blow if it meant the blow was real.

From the back somewhere comes a commotion. You turn, grateful and relieved for any distraction.

"This is the most stupid test ever! I hate it! I hate this class! I hate everyone!"

Kevin has stood up, scrunched up his worksheet, and thrown it across the room. The paper ball comes to a rolling stop by your ankle.

"Kevin! Please go to the principal's office. How many times do I have to tell you about your behavior?" Miss Cicely looks beaten, ill-equipped to deal with this.

Kevin marches straight out the door without saying a thing, his shoulders hunched and his thumbs in his pockets. You have a vague recollection of a shy boy in his cartoon-character robe, which does not fit in with this angry boy in front of you. Some of your classmates snicker and whisper to one another. A certain girl and her friends shake their heads.

You pick up the paper ball and unwrap it. You find that he has three answers right and twelve answers wrong.

Well, at least he did much better than you.

In that case, since you did much worse, you should be screaming and overturning desks and flipping over chairs. This you imagine in your mind, and to your surprise, you find it satisfying. But your real body sits there obedient and small. As always.

"Put that in the trash," Miss Cicely snaps. You hastily scrunch the paper ball back up and drop it in the basket by your teacher's desk.

"I don't know why it's so hard," you overhear your former friend say. "He must have rocks in his head."

You have no idea what that term means, except that it sounds very painful and you feel ignorant once again.

During lunchtime Kevin Huynh, a ball of nervous and angry energy, decides to push a kid over for seemingly no reason. The saddest thing is that the kid is just a quiet bespectacled boy reading a comic on a bench, trying to keep to himself. You can see in Kevin's face that he regrets it as soon as he does it, but the teacher on lunch duty shakes him by the arm and off to the principal's office he goes again.

Part of his punishment is to stand against the painted wall that faces the grass quadrangle with the flagpole in the middle. He will stand there, forfeiting his playtime, until the bell rings for class to begin again. Then the principal will see him. Maybe on other days the painted wall fills up with the worst offenders the school has to offer, but today Kevin is the only one there. Hands behind his back, his legs kicking at the concrete in front of him.

You try to think about what the principal is like, but all you imagine is something faceless and horrible and cruel.

At first you stand on the other side of the quadrangle staring at Kevin. Then you move closer by standing underneath the covered assembly area. Then you are almost within touching distance of the wall. In an effort to brighten up the old school the wall has been absurdly painted with slogans in big bubble writing—HIP TO BE A SQUARE, THE RAD 80S! and PHONE HOME—none of which makes sense to you, so the wall actually seems more threatening.

Why you have slowly inched this far and pretended you have been standing still on the spot all this time is a question with an answer that eludes you. You suspect you are trying to make friends with a bad boy. A boy Ma Ma would never agree for you to be friends with if she saw how he behaved, even if he is Mrs. Huynh's son. Maybe that is exactly why you are doing it. Maybe you are hoping some of his attitude will rub off on you.

"I really think the problems started when they

banned using the cane at this school," says an adult voice.

The two teachers coming out of the faculty lounge see you and Kevin and quickly say no more. You don't think you were supposed to hear their conversation. You find yourself pressed next to Kevin's side, even though you are not even in trouble. You are hoping to melt into the wall. You look guilty of something.

"What language are you two speaking?" one of the teachers says, even though neither of you is talking.

"You need to speak the language that everyone speaks in this country," the teacher continues, as if saying this only because the other teacher is there.

You want to tell the teacher that you can't understand Kevin's language anyway and he doesn't understand yours, but you feel you have to keep your mouth shut.

"We've said nothing," Kevin replies. "We were reading each other's minds, and since that's silent, who cares what language we do it in?"

The teacher frowns at Kevin, looks at the punishment wall that this mouthy kid is already standing at, and then shakes his head. The teachers leave without saying anything more to either of you, their heads pressed together in adult whispers. Kevin kicks the wall and makes a black shoe mark there.

"Have you come to laugh at me?" Kevin says loudly. "I saw you watching me all this time, you know."

You are not laughing. You have been doing your best not to cry.

"I don't care if the principal is allowed to use the cane on me or not," he says defiantly. "My father will beat me with the stick end of his plastic fly-swatter when he gets home! Or maybe he won't because I've stashed it away. By the time he grabs a flip-flop instead, I will have found a good place to hide."

Kevin laughs in a scary fashion. You still don't laugh.

"Hello. It's a nice day to be out in the winter sun, isn't it?"

You both turn toward the voice and then instinctively step away, even though you shouldn't have to be scared of teachers.

This teacher, though, is the nicest-looking human you have ever seen. She has eyes that are blue like the sky and a half-moon of a pink smile. She has the permed hair of a princess. On her collar is pinned a brooch of a human heart, studded with rubies and bloodred stones.

"You must be Meixing. Good to meet you. I'm Heather Jardine. You can call me Ms. Jardine." She crouches down so she is at the same level as you. "Good to see you too, Kevin, yes, I am very well myself, thanks for asking."

Kevin grunts and kicks the wall. You become anxious that Ms. Jardine is calling him out for something wrong—you aren't even sure why you feel anxious for him; it's like you feel anxious for everybody these days—until you see that she is smiling and that Kevin is giving her some sort of half smile back. They are joking. You think. It's confusing.

"There's a new program that the school is setting up. I thought I'd talk to you both about it. For an hour each day you will have class with me. We will work on learning new words, reading, and writing. How does that sound?"

"She definitely needs it," says Kevin, pointing at you. "She doesn't know the language at all. As for me, I'm just stupid. Ask anyone you like! No one believes in me, anyway."

"I believe in you," replies Ms. Jardine.

This catches Kevin off guard. An expression of genuine surprise fills his face before he goes back to scowling.

The bell rings.

"I'll see you both for the first class soon," says Ms. Jardine. "I really look forward to it."

You do too. You look down at your hands. Through the tears in your eyes, the colors of the wall look like a rainbow.

CHAPTER TEN

Book

❧✦❧

Your heart fills your entire mouth as soon as you reach home after the school day. You look up at Big Scary looming large in front of you, her too-green cactus stems still pinned to the walls like surprised fingers pressed against her face.

The eye in the Room on the Roof winks. Once. But it doesn't make you feel any better, as you are so anxious about your mother. You shouldn't have left her. But you are just a child and she ordered you to go to school. But what if something bad has happened? You trudge up the thirty steps.

Ma Ma is strangely . . . okay. She is talking animatedly on the phone. When she hangs up, she tells you Second Aunty is making arrangements to come and stay for a while. Then she is on the phone again, talking to other family members back home. It is strange to see her so alive, excited almost.

An arrangement of fresh vegetables in a cardboard box—the ones Mrs. Huynh brings around, with the words on the side that are neither the Old nor the New Language—sits on the floor and there is a wok on the stovetop. There are some sliced vegetables on the chopping board and an opened can of baby corn spears. For the first time since she got here, Ma Ma is preparing dinner.

She doesn't talk about Ba Ba. She concentrates on keeping herself busy, doing multiple things at once, and being more attentive and interested in cooking and housework—pointing out cobwebs that First Uncle the bachelor hadn't dusted—than she has since arriving.

Ma Ma looks as big as the moon. You don't think she should be trying to do so much. You are sure Mrs. Huynh will tell her not to do so much. Ba Ba didn't like her doing so much—well, he didn't like it yesterday, anyway. *Slow down and be sad with me,* you want to say, tears in the edges of your eyes. But Ma Ma does what she likes, moving determinedly around with her belly out front. The only thing she can't do is look you in the eye; in fact, she cannot look at you at all. You are acknowledged as there, but invisible at the same time. You wish she would stop and see you. You wish she would ask you how school was, if you had a good day.

In turn, you want to tell her it's not her fault that Ba Ba drove out last night. It's not her fault that she had an opinion and got into an argument. It's not her fault because you can remember her voice calling him back, but Ba Ba walked out that door anyway. You don't blame her for anything. The police had explained to you clearly that it was an accident and had checked to make sure that part was understood by both of you.

Yet, you cannot reach her. Ma Ma is still there, but disappeared within herself. You don't know how to get her back.

With your burlap bag almost falling off your slumped shoulder, you trudge down the steps into the backyard. The black-and-white cat greets you. In fact, she stands up on her hind feet and gives you a bow. In return, you have no choice but to bow back.

The long grass sways in greeting, each blade like a subject in your kingdom, cheering for their approaching queen, although it is hard to see the individual blades when everything becomes soft and blurred through your tears.

You greet your broken glasshouse as though it is your greatest friend. Maybe it understands what it's like to look damaged on the outside but to be brimming with the hopes and dreams of an entire universe inside.

First Uncle is where you left him, standing on his wooden stepladder in his orchard, except the weather has changed and he has put on his favorite sweater. The one in the photo that he sent with his last letter, so that you would all recognize him when he came to pick you up during the airport run that never came to pass.

The sun, climbing to the middle of the sky, smiles down at you with a sweet, serene expression, the rays around her face like a golden crown. The waxing moon, with part of her face hidden like a lady wearing a large-brimmed hat, has her eyes closed and is sleeping peacefully.

"Where are you buried?" you ask Uncle. "You didn't invite us to your funeral."

"I didn't have one. I was cremated without any ceremony whatsoever and then had a tree planted on top of me in honor. Guess what type of tree?"

"Does it happen to be an orange tree?"

"You're a smart kid."

Ma Ma had mumbled something to you once, before you came here, about how she liked the idea of you getting a New Land education, but she wasn't sure she wanted you to get any other funny New Land ideas. This is perhaps what she meant.

"Do you want to plant another seed?"

You nod and eagerly lift open his giant seed box. This time you select a much larger seed, dark brown and shiny; it sits in the middle of your palm like a coat button.

Beside your field of blue flowers, you plant the seed, pat the soil, and give it a gentle watering. Everything in the glasshouse inhales and exhales at the same time, then begins to breathe. From the soil comes a shoot that shakes herself free and determinedly grows until she becomes a tree. Years pass in the blink of an eye, and she becomes tall, strong, and green.

Then, all of a sudden, all the leaves drop off.

The tree becomes completely bare. You feel how she feels. Overnight you lost everything too.

But then thousands of soft little buds form at the tips of all her branches.

And then she flowers.

From the branches, masses of downturned blue flowers weep all the way to the ground. When you touch the smooth, twisting trunk, you know that the tree is only following the cycle of life. She knows your thoughts and your sadness and she tells you that it's okay to feel these things. One day you will become flowers too.

"Ah," says First Uncle. "A blue Chinese wisteria. A fine choice of ornamental tree. It looks very lovely."

The pink serpent slithers up the trunk and tangles itself in the flowers. It hisses at you; makes you think of the girls at school. Although you are concerned it might be venomous, it is also candy pink, so you are not afraid of it.

Underneath the sun and the moon and the curved glass ceiling, sitting with your back against the wisteria tree, you take your worksheet out of your burlap bag. In the absence of a cane on the palm of your hand because it is not allowed anymore, or a chicken feather duster on the back of your legs because you don't have a father anymore, it's as if you need to look at those fifteen red crosses to punish yourself. You stare down at the paper and sigh.

A tear falls and turns one of the crosses into a little red galaxy before the whole thing slides off the page completely. And with that, something extraordinary happens. All the other wrong answers and gibberish words and sentences you don't understand get up and walk off the page, never to be seen again. You stare at the blank page in wonder, like it's telling you there is a possibility to start again. The piece of paper suddenly darkens so that only a little rectangle lights up, like a tiny cinema screen.

What it shows you is a much older girl, a teenager with long legs and a short skirt, sitting under a tree in summer . . . like the tree you're sitting against now. Except the tree is older and wiser and the flowers have all turned purple.

She is reading a fat novel, one with long words, thin pages, and no pictures. The slight smile on her face indicates that she is lost within the pages; lost within her own world. You marvel at the peace she's surrounded by, the contentedness she has created for herself, before you wonder if you've seen her before. She does look vaguely familiar . . .

Maybe she is one of your many cousins, whom you have only seen in photos.

But none of your cousins has a freckle under her left eye like this girl does. What Ma Ma and her sisters call a "bad luck beauty mark" because it means the owner will always weep. But you have often wondered in times of quiet reflection if it is okay for someone to cry throughout their entire life story if that's the way they feel and if it gets them through in the end to become a stronger person.

None of your cousins is marked like this. Only you.

The scene of the paper cinema changes, and the same girl is now getting up on a stage and shaking hands with a woman who looks thrilled to be handing her a certificate and a wrapped present. The girl squints into the audience, but it is hard to see under the bright lights. All she knows is that everyone is clapping and some people are standing in their seats and someone takes her photo because it is a great achievement.

You can't read what is written on the certificate, but the girl is smiling and covering her mouth in surprise, and it is only many years later, when it all happens to you, for real, that you understand what it says:

PREMIER'S SHORT STORY WRITING CONTEST

OVERALL STATE HIGH SCHOOL WINNER:

MEIXING LIM

CHAPTER ELEVEN

Paper Clip

T he following days are weird and frightening, in the sense that they merge into one monster of a nightmare, yet each of them are individually terrible, as though the monster has different faces. Ma Ma preoccupies herself with pulling out what appears to be an endless supply of bedding and bath towels from Big Scary's linen closet as she readies herself for guests. The washing machine is on all hours of the morning and evening, and even when you are at school, you imagine it still spinning.

Perhaps the loud clanging sound of the ancient machine helps to drown out the thoughts in both your heads. All you know is that every morning Ma Ma is trying to ignore you by not being around. You dress yourself, defrost a breakfast *bao* in the microwave, and place the lunch Mrs. Huynh has packed for you in your burlap bag. From the top of the back step, you stand and watch Ma Ma hang out the laundry, the cold winter wind pushing the sheets up and flapping them about like ghosts.

One very early morning Ailing is the first to arrive. She is the youngest of all your aunts, except you are not allowed to called her Aunty. You have to call her by her first name only, Ailing. It doesn't really make any sense because, out of courtesy, you are forced to call all manner of people who aren't related to you Aunty, like Mrs. Huynh next door.

You know that Ailing was given upon birth to your Ah Ma's best friend, Madam Pearl, who had watched from her big beautiful house up at Dragon's Tail as Ah Ma gave birth to one son and seven daughters and then an eighth daughter, all the while Madam Pearl remaining childless herself. Ma Ma had always told you in a flippant manner that Ah Ma gave Ailing away to maintain the friendship and to stop Madam Pearl from getting even more jealous. You think that maybe Ma Ma is jealous, as Ailing grew up rich, has had an expensive education in a Fancy Faraway Land, and doesn't need a man to look after her.

Ailing, though, has the saddest eyes you have ever seen. You have a feeling it's not only because of Ba Ba's passing, but because she is always sad. She goes to put her arms around Ma Ma and give her a kiss on the cheek, because that is the custom from the Fancy Faraway Land, but Ma Ma pulls away awkwardly, because Ma Ma is very Old Land.

Ailing is busy as soon as she's inside and has access to a phone, talking to the funeral home, settling legal matters, and organizing flights for your other six Aunties in her gentle voice that speaks the New Language perfectly, but somehow differently at the same time. Like how she asks Ma Ma if she has any breakfast "yog-gurt" and it takes you a while to realize she is asking for "yo-gurt," the little tubs you've seen in lunch boxes at school. Ma Ma does not know either way since she's never heard of such a food.

"Do you want me to invite anyone from your husband's side?" Ailing asks Ma Ma, switching easily back to the Old Language.

"No," Ma Ma says firmly with her mouth in a straight line.

"Do you think this will cause drama?"

"There is already enough drama within our family for an entire Peking opera."

"That is true."

"It is my husband, my rules."

Ailing purses her lips, shrugs, and goes to open the pantry. She takes out flour and, from the very back, a container of baking powder, which she shakes. The lump at the bottom of the container doesn't move. You don't know how long that baking powder has been in the pantry, a stray leftover from First Uncle perhaps.

Eggs are cracked and milk splashed and Ailing is cooking fragrant round disks in a frying pan. You don't know why, but you feel instantly comforted.

"Pancakes," says Ailing, and she slides one onto a plate for you. It is very good. You hope for another.

Ma Ma stares at Ailing as if she is a new species of alien. Then she bends over with great difficulty and takes out the great big metal steamer from the cupboard.

"I'm going to teach you to make *kueh*," she says to Ailing.

You love *kueh*. Your mouth waters at the thought of biting into those sweet, chewy pieces of tapioca. You hope it is the nine-layer rainbow one.

"Using Ah Ma's special recipe," says Ma Ma. "No one has a better recipe, not even the sellers at the *pasar malam*."

Ailing's eyes soften and take on a wistful look as she thinks of the desserts at the night market.

You want to stay behind and hang around your aunt like a dog hangs around a person it has taken to, but you've learned your lesson about asking to stay home on a school day. You wave a shy goodbye to Ailing. She smiles and tells you to have a nice day. This small but kind gesture that Ma Ma has never indulged you with makes you feel good on the inside.

Ailing eyes your burlap bag and her mouth makes a funny twitch, but you hope that she can see it's only because Ma Ma can't afford anything better, not because you are being neglected.

That afternoon your schedule at school changes. Miss Cicely tells you and Kevin to step out of the class and report to Ms. Jardine's room. A spark of excitement like a miniature firework explodes in the darkness inside you, and you stand up like a shot. As you both make your way to the door, all eyes in the classroom are on you and you start to feel embarrassed. Your former friend whispers with the other girls, and they break out in tiny laughter.

"They are *lovers*," you hear her say. "Both as dumb as each other! Going to special class together!"

You wish that Miss Cicely would tell your former friend to be quiet and not to talk out of turn, as those are Miss Cicely's rules, but your teacher likes your friend. That is because she is everything you are not: spirited, confident, and poised. You pull a frown and hurry out of the classroom, putting a wide space between you and Kevin.

Kevin tries to walk alongside you, but you keep hurrying on ahead. When you realize you don't know the direction to Ms. Jardine's room, you slow down and start trailing behind. He stops walking to allow you to catch up. You stop as well and refuse to walk while he isn't walking. He scowls at you.

That is why it takes you by surprise when he suddenly turns around and marches right up to you. You look around in desperation, but you have no choice but to stand where you are, as running away from him would be plain embarrassing. You will have to take the consequences of playing the silly game you started. He stops in front of you, takes hold of your wrist, makes you open your hand, and drops your Ah Ma's gold ring in your palm.

You stare at him, speechless as usual, but more so, as even the words inside your head, of all the things you want to say, have disappeared.

"I stole it back off her before class this morning."

You stand there like a statue.

"So do you want it or not?" he says irritably.

You close your hand around the ring and drop your arm by your side. *Thank you,* you mouth.

That is how you end up walking side by side over the green lawn and around the school lake, to a rickety old portable classroom standing on wooden legs.

A huge mound of mulch beside it seems to have been there so long, it has solidified into a mountain.

Kevin marches straight in without hesitation and you linger by the doorway, allowing yourself to look by pretending you are not looking at anything.

It's so pleasant and inviting. Shelves line the back of the classroom, brimming with books. There is a round rug, tufted with many different shaggy colors, and beanbag chairs around it.

Sitting inside already, at one of the desks arranged into a small circle instead of rows, is the boy you recognize as the shy, comic-reading kid who Kevin had pushed in the assembly area that one time at lunch. Kevin sits down next to him without thinking this might make the boy uncomfortable or scared. But the boy doesn't look fazed; his tongue sticks out the corner of his mouth as he concentrates on the work in front of him.

"Hello and welcome," says Ms. Jardine. She is wearing a different brooch—this one is of a hand, completely white with seed pearls except for a red line of stones at the bottom where it is severed.

"Meet Josh Khoury. Meixing, come and sit down with us."

It is cold inside, but you don't care because of the warmth of your teacher.

"Thank you, Miss Jardine," you say, careful to

pronounce your words slowly and clearly.

"I'm actually a Ms.," she says, and smiles.

"What does *it*—that mean?"

"It's like a Mr. Instead of being a Miss or a Mrs., I don't know why women can't all be a Ms. Does anyone really need to know if a woman is married or not? Does that make her better or worse or any different? No one in this school agrees with me, but oh well!"

Ms. Jardine laughs in good humor.

You take an empty seat next to her.

It feels a little strange, as you really think she should be at the front of the class, but here she is sitting with you as if she were a student too.

"So, I would like each of you to tell me a bit about yourself. What are your interests? What do you hope to achieve in this class? Your hopes and dreams?"

Josh goes first. He says that he likes stories, but because no one in his family can read and as he himself did not start to speak the New Language until last year, he can't read very well. That's why he likes comics, because anyone can understand pictures. You find yourself nodding along.

Josh is working on drawing his own original comic where the hero has the superpower of knowing everything because he has read every book ever written. Ms. Jardine is helping him with the words.

Josh says he hopes that he can graduate to the next grade at the end of this year, as he was held back a year last time.

Kevin is supposed to go next, but he refuses to say anything about himself. He folds his arms and says the class is a stupid idea and he is not sure why he got picked because nothing is going to help him. He says he doesn't have any hopes and dreams because it gives people stupid ideas, like thinking they can fly when they can't and falling off a roof and breaking their arm.

You get the feeling that maybe when Kevin was younger, he tied a towel around his shoulders and made his way to the top of his house. But you don't say anything. Ms. Jardine passes him a stack of colored paper and asks him to draw how he feels.

It is your turn, and you wonder about showing Ms. Jardine the last picture book you drew. The one you thought about throwing away, along with the mangy old eraser and stubs of colored pencils in your ziplock bag, because you are still downhearted that it wasn't what Miss Cicely wanted from you. But you couldn't do it. It is a piece of you.

You slide the little book out and across the desk to Ms. Jardine. She opens it and looks through the pages. You might not be ready to talk in this class, even though it is just your teacher and the two boys, but you're ready to show her a bit of your heart.

Ms. Jardine smiles as she carefully looks at all the pages.

She turns to the last page and sees the drawing that you did completely in blue pencil. She points to the blue girl. You pat the spot over your heart.

"Is everything okay at home?" Ms. Jardine asks, searching your face with her eyes.

You nod even before you think about the question properly.

"You know you can always talk to me, all right?"

You nod quickly again.

With her neat hand, on a new sheet of paper, she writes: *Glasshouse. Sun. Moon. Sky. Seed. Serpent. Orange trees. Blue. Grow. Learn. Thrive.*

She reads the words out to you and then looks them up in the big dictionary she takes off the shelf filled with books. She asks you to copy the words, and you do so with enthusiasm, feeling for the first time that you are learning something, that you aren't stupid or unable to keep up with an entire class that already knows so much more than you. You write the words out and you write them again, because the act of making the shapes of the letters with your pencil gives you great joy.

Ms. Jardine gives you another page of words to copy.

"That's an activity for preschoolers," Kevin scoffs as he looks at you, but you take no notice. You feel satisfied with yourself. Your heart feels quite full.

"I've got one for big boys," says Ms. Jardine without a fuss, and hands him an activity with lots of words. "See if you can read all those sentences and then draw what they say."

Kevin says, "Of course I can!" and "It'll be a cinch!" and he falls quiet.

You look over at Josh and watch as he draws his hero sticking a paper clip into a lock. He sees you looking and explains.

"Book Boy got put into a cell by the baddies, but since he uses a paper clip for a bookmark, he's using it to pick his way out. He always carries a book around. The baddies didn't think a book could be a weapon, but little did they know!"

You give him a shy smile. You think a paper clip is a marvelous invention.

Josh gives you a smile back.

"I can't quite draw the lock right, though," he adds, pressing his pencil against his lips.

You take a blank piece of paper from Ms. Jardine's pile and try sketching one yourself.

"Yours looks heaps better than mine. Can I draw it like yours?"

You nod.

"Thanks!" In return, Josh slides a blue coloring pencil across your desk.

"You can have it, it's a spare. I noticed that yours is only a stub. You must use it a lot, huh?"

You nod again. Josh doesn't seem to mind that you don't have any words to say.

The silence is interrupted by a yell. Kevin is standing up, tearing at the activity Ms. Jardine had given him, as if it has personally attacked him.

"Come with me," says Ms. Jardine, and she leads him outside. Both you and Josh rush to the door and look out curiously. You watch as by the lake your teacher picks rocks from the ground and hands them to Kevin, who tosses them into the water one by one, as hard as he can.

Exhausted, Kevin eventually squats down onto the dirt and starts crying. Absolutely howling. Ms. Jardine stands patiently beside him and lets him get it out of his system.

You and Josh hurry back to your seats as they come back in and pretend you have been working all this time. Kevin sits down. Ms. Jardine sits down next to him. She gets Kevin to read out the words on the page to her. Whenever he stumbles and gets angry, she puts a calming hand on his arm and asks him to try again. He makes it to the end of the page. Ms. Jardine gives him a round of applause. Kevin pretends not to care, but you know he does. You can see it in his eyes, his body, his whole being.

It is then you understand that Kevin isn't angry at the world; he's angry at himself.

The time flies and you are sorry to leave Ms. Jardine's class, but you take heart in the knowledge that you will be back tomorrow. Each day, for one hour.

"I want to eventually see you put all the words to the pictures in your story," Ms. Jardine tells you. You do too. There is so much swirling inside your head. You can feel that wisteria tree twisting inside your soul. One day all the words in your head will connect with the pen in your fingers, and it will come spilling out like flowers from their buds. You will become a writer.

CHAPTER TWELVE
Olives

When school lets out on this particular day, you don't wait for random strangers to group around the road crossing. Warming your hands with puffs of your breath, you stand by the utility pole where the yellow flyers have been repasted, waiting for the same boy to come tear them down again. You look at the ring on your finger. He doesn't show up. Josh, though, walks past you with his nose in another comic book, and you try not to show the disappointment on your face when he stops to talk to you.

"Where do you live?"

You point at the crossing and then walk your fingers through the air to the right.

"I go that way too. Do you want to walk together?"

Josh adjusts his glasses and squints at one of the yellow flyers, looks at the badly drawn face with the slits for eyes, the triangle hat, crooked teeth, and single plait of hair.

You are embarrassed for whoever drew it since they are such a poor artist when Josh is such a good one.

You stab your finger on the words and look at Josh expectantly.

"I don't know what the first word is. It might be slang, and I don't know all slang words yet—they are the hardest to learn," says Josh. "But the rest says, 'go back home.'"

Josh becomes silent. Then he carefully tears the flyers off the pole and slides them into a nearby trash bin. "We don't need to bother with them. Let's go."

"Your speaking is so good" are the first-ever words you say to him.

He notices that you exhale deeply and your shoulders slump.

"I've had a whole year to speak the language. I bet this time next year you will be speaking much better too. You don't think so now, but you will."

Josh gives you two thumbs up.

You lift your hanging head and give him two thumbs up back.

Together you walk home side by side. When you cross the road after the Lollipop Man blows his whistle and spreads out his flags, you watch as Josh glances over to give him a broad grin. You watch as Josh gives him the same thumbs-up sign. In a sudden spontaneous moment that lights you up, you are filled with the optimism that you could also be as free and generous with your feelings. For the first time you acknowledge the Lollipop Man by giving him a thumbs-up too. You want to learn the local customs; you want to be part of this. The old man looks surprised, then he gives you a smile back.

At the front of Big Scary you tug at your new friend's arm to let him know that this is your house. Josh opens his mouth and stares from the bottom step to the roofline. You follow the same path with your eyes. When you reach the top, you see a triangle roof, filled in with concrete with a semicircle design in the center. There is no Room on the Roof; there is no window; there is no eye. You look over at Josh and you believe that is what he is seeing.

Perhaps Big Scary is wary of strangers. What you want to say to her is that you hope she stops being shy and acts like her true self, because you want Josh to be your friend who comes over to visit all the time. You suddenly want to show Josh something. You find yourself grabbing on to his wrist and pulling him toward the rickety red side gate, the heart-shaped eyes staring at you, the padlock falling to pieces as you pull against one of the pickets.

Josh bends like a piece of bamboo—like someone who is used to being led around—and he doesn't question it when you drag him out to the backyard.

There the black-and-white cat is walking forward to greet you on her hind feet. You can see her little face bobbing above the grass. You let go of Josh and make him look at the cat face-to-face to see if he can see what you see.

He stares at the cat for the longest time. The cat stares back at him with an unfazed, dour face.

Finally, he says, "How did you teach your cat to stand up on her back legs like a human?"

You want to interrupt and say she's not your cat, but you let him continue.

"And how did you teach her to hold a tray of drinks?"

You laugh in delight then. You take the two glasses of fresh orange juice from the cat, and you bow deeply to her while she bows deeply back. Josh takes the glass you hand him with wonder and suspicion, but he has a sip anyway. You take hold of his sleeve and lead him to the glasshouse. He has a right to frown as a pane in the roof randomly cracks and falls inward.

Taking hold of the door handle and beckoning for him to follow, you squeeze your eyes tight as you slip in, feeling him follow behind.

You don't dare open your eyes until you hear the gasp escape from Josh. Then you feel your face relax under the warmth of the sun, now high in the sky. The conventions you are bound by in the normal world disappear, and you smile to see your world of orange trees, endless blue, and forget-me-not fields. Like a book of black-and-white drawings you are filling in with your favorite colors. The moon in the sky has become a crescent, so she wears a veil on the part of her face that has disappeared.

"What is this place?" Josh exclaims.

"You see it too?"

Josh nods quietly.

You call out for First Uncle, but First Uncle does not appear to be there. Perhaps he has gone out shopping. You lead Josh to the precious box of seeds, and you open the lid and indicate that he can take one. He takes a long time to choose, as he seems to be looking for something in particular, frowning behind his glasses. Then his face eases, he smiles, and he shows you the seed in his palm, sad-looking and wrinkled as though it is already old.

Together you help Josh plant and water the seed.

Then you both quietly stand back and finish drinking your juice.

The wind in the glasshouse quietly blows, your forget-me-nots flutter, and your blue wisteria tree gently sways. Then from the damp soil the first shoot pushes through. As it moves and dances up toward the rays of the sun, it tells you a story.

You see a large family in a foreign country, and huddled among them is a boy you recognize as a younger Josh. He has lost a lens out of his glasses. But it looks as though he has no choice but to wear the broken pair, as there is no replacement in sight.

As the first leaf appears on the shoot, you see an entire building crumble and turn to dust. As the young plant gains more leaves and pushes the sky away, you see the largest sea of people you have ever seen all moving in one direction; snaking into a single file as the dust road narrows.

You want to know where they are all going, but you have the feeling that they don't really know either, and your stomach hurts. You search frantically for Josh, as suddenly he's not next to you anymore, but lost somewhere in the mass. In relief you see him clinging to the back of his father like a scared monkey. Mostly he has to walk for himself, though, like everyone else. The lens is still missing from his glasses.

The seedling has now become a young tree, but it is still growing. You see so many rows of tents. So many borders and roads; so much hunger and heat. The young tree grows into a strong tree, and out of the blue you see an airplane and feel a sense of hope. You see Josh and his family strapped into seats. The words "I've been there too!" jump into your throat, and you promise him in your mind that where he is going, he will be able to get a new lens for his glasses.

The tree has now finished flowering, and the small clusters of white blossoms lose their petals and become green fruit that slowly turns a deep, shiny shade of black. You turn your head and the Josh of today is by your side, a pair of large square glasses—that contain both lenses—balanced on his nose. He has a sad look on his face, but it is also thoughtful and reflective.

"Back home we had olive trees that were six thousand years old."

Home. It is such a confusing word for you, as it could mean the village your family came from, or it could be that island home in the middle that you liked best, or it could be this home Uncle left you. When people ask you, "Where are you from?" you genuinely have no idea what to say.

Josh pulls an olive off the tree and you do as well, rolling the hard fruit between your fingers. Then you pop the thing in your mouth and bite down.

You do not expect there to be a stone in the middle, and that is what your teeth painfully crack upon. Which wouldn't be so bad if not for the fact that the flavor flooding your mouth is the most awful and bitter thing you have ever tasted. You quickly spit it out and ground the remains into the dirt with your foot. You glance up to see Josh give you a horrified look.

"If I had known you were going to eat it raw, I would have warned you not to."

You turn red and cover your mouth.

A smile breaks out on Josh's face and he covers his mouth too. The boy has the nerve to laugh at you! You turn your face away and try to gracefully spit out the rest of the taste in your mouth, and you find yourself grinning too. Then you belly laugh at yourself. It comes to you in a tidal wave of tears and snot, and you wipe it away.

"My story is the same as millions of other people," says Josh, sounding sad. "But don't worry about me. You should come around to my place sometime, and my mom can let you eat the olives she preserves from our garden. You might like those better."

Smiling back at him, you take his hand in gratitude and he gives your palm a squeeze. The olive tree shakes its leaves out, thankful for having been released from a seed so small.

You want to show Ma Ma you have made a friend, so you both climb the twenty-six steps to the back door and you instruct him to take his shoes off before he enters the house. It turns out he doesn't wear shoes inside his house either. Maybe you are more similar than you think.

"Hello, Mrs. Lim," he says to Ma Ma.

"*Aunty,*" you correct him.

"Aunty," he corrects himself, and then to Ailing he says, "And hello to you, too, Aunty."

"I'm just Ailing," she replies.

"Ailing," he echoes.

Adjusting to different cultures is confusing enough without family politics and drama, you think.

Ailing doesn't seem fazed by this brown-colored boy you have brought into the house as she eats her way through the family-sized tub of yogurt she has gotten her hands on. This is probably because Ailing has traveled all around the world and seen everybody. Ma Ma, on the other hand, is giving Josh the longest stare.

Cautiously, she pushes a plate of warm, steamed dumplings under his nose.

Josh stares at them and just as cautiously takes one. He puts it in his mouth and chews it carefully. A surprised look fills his face and he smiles. Then his hand reaches for another.

"Eat away! That's the best way to your future mother-in-law's heart," Ailing says. It makes your face turn red, but your aunt's eyes are mischievous and dancing.

Ma Ma is pleased with her empty plate. She peels two Granny Smith apples, salts them, and pushes them whole onto forks. She gives you one each and you drag Josh away. You both munch on the salty and sweet crispy apple, and you show him all the empty rooms of Big Scary. As you go, you count the thirteen different types of tiles she wears and the four different types of fur. Big Scary remains passive about the whole experience and doesn't have anything extra to show. You think about the pale pink door she showed you once that had a playground behind it, and you get a funny twinge in your heart, but you have to let that go.

You point out your bedroom with its pink bed frame and one pink square wall, but there is no pink light from the wardrobe, as it is daytime. Hastily, you hide your rag doll under the pillow and hope he didn't see it. You show him the alcove you like to sit inside and daydream.

"Do you want to draw?" you ask him hopefully, but Josh says he has to go home or else his mother will get worried.

"She worries all the time. She still has nightmares about that one time when we got accidentally separated. She's better about it now, but . . ." He trails off, looking forlornly at the apple core sitting on his fork.

You watch Josh leave and you find yourself feeling a little empty. All the furniture in the front room seems to shrink to half its size, and the house feels empty too.

You glance up at the cream-colored wall. From deep inside, Big Scary pulses in pink three times quickly, three times slowly, and then three times quickly again, which you recognize as a code she is trying to send but which you can't quite grasp.

Back up in your bedroom, tucked inside the alcove that fits you snugly, you take out your colored pencils and start drawing. You make a story about a girl who meets a boy and they become friends. The story ends with them playing on a space rocket, heading toward the stars, because you like happy endings; you want your characters to be happy living inside your books. Stapling the pages together, you feel a happy feeling inside your heart, but at the same time you feel the loneliness more than before. You are certain that if Josh stayed longer, you would have been able to open up. You look at the happy faces in your book.

CHAPTER THIRTEEN

Wolfberries

ᑐᑐᑐ

With as much noise and fuss as possible, your six other Aunties arrive. On a rainy Friday morning they bring with them sweet mung bean cookies, dried ingredients to make herbal soups, and cartoon-printed pajamas for you from the *pasar malam* back home. They are counterfeit, of course, with HELLO TTKIY printed on them, but they are real pajamas and you love them. Most importantly of all, your Aunties bring a breath of loud, fresh air.

They want to know if you can speak the New Language yet, have you become a New Citizen, and has your skin changed color accordingly. "You look white," they say as they compare arms with you. They want to know why it is so cold. When it will stop raining. Where to buy seasonal vegetables, a bigger rice cooker, five pounds of chicken wings and a whole chicken. There are six of them, but they all speak like one beast. Six heads, but only one voice.

Standing there, grouped together like big and small steps, are your cousins, from seventeen-year-old Biaoge, looking deeply uncomfortable, to little Biaomei, grinning at you with a smile of mystery and mischief.

Ailing drives First and Second Aunty to the shops in the van she's rented, and it is not long before the scent of jasmine white rice fills the air, large mixing bowls are heaped with turmeric-dipped chicken wings, and a whole chicken is simmering away with wolfberries and red dates. The latter is for Ma Ma, who First Aunty describes in her expert medical opinion, when she places a hand on your mother's forehead, as "heaty." You want to correct First Aunty and tell her it's just Ma Ma's bad temper and that it's her new personality since she became pregnant, but you must respect Aunty, so you say nothing.

You sneak a look at Ma Ma through the crack in her bedroom door, but instead of being stony and silent, she is sitting on the bed with a slight smile on her face, folding laundry and humming to herself. It is clear that she is happy that everyone is here, even if they are pushy and noisy. The pile of blankets obscures her large tummy, and looking at her profile, she appears young and radiant. At a glance she could be Ailing, a free agent and much maligned, but her own person all the same. You wonder why Ma Ma left her family in the first place.

Quietly, you inch away and quickly go up the secret spiral staircase to the second floor, where the noise of your aunts, calling to one another from different ends of the house, drowns out the thoughts in your head about the past and the future and brings you back to the present.

"So this is what life affords you when you're the only son of the family," says one Aunty.

"And therefore the only one to get an education," says another.

"Stop speaking ill of the dead—that is such bad luck," scolds the voice you clearly recognize as belonging to First Aunty. "He paid for all your children's tuition fees, so shut up."

"You'd think he was an emperor, wouldn't you?" pipes up one remaining voice you think belongs to Sixth Aunty.

You know the house has many bedrooms, but you didn't realize it has *this* many. Big Scary seems to grow to accommodate, even though the offerings are simple. Most of the rooms are furnished with only sheeted mattresses on the floor. Your aunts do not mind; they say they are used to it being like this back home. Your older cousins sit around, swap comics, and pretend to be unfazed. Biaoge silently ponders the obligations of his role as the firstborn boy in the family tree.

The bathrooms must have multiplied as well. You are glad that Big Scary thought to factor this in. Although your aunts tell Ma Ma that they are ever so grateful, not to fuss, and that everything is fine, you know that it is really only some politeness clause in your cultural contract; if your aunts had to wait to have a shower or to sit on the toilet, you wouldn't hear the end of it!

Sitting side by side on a queen-sized mattress in one room, looking around curiously, are the two daughters of Fourth Aunty, Lifen and Lihua. You are not allowed to call them by their real names, of course, but by their titles, Biaojie and Biaomei. One year older and one year younger than you, respectively. They are dressed in identical stiff satin dresses because this was their first plane trip too, so it was a big deal. They both look as though they can't wait to take them off.

You stand in the doorway and look at them, and they stare back at you. You haven't seen them before; they are strangers to you. You were born on your island home and your parents couldn't afford to go back to the Old Land because they were busy saving all their money for the New Land. You feel shy, but Biaomei pats the space on the mattress next to her. You go and sit down.

"What is school like here? Is it so much better than the school we have at home?" says Biaomei.

"I heard if you go to school here, you can grow up to be anything, because it is a land of the free—is that true?" says Biaojie.

Suddenly, they have so many questions for you that you can't really answer because all this time you've been in survival mode. You've been kicking so hard at the deep water you've been thrown in, trying to float, that you haven't thought about swimming, let alone noticed how great the pool is supposed to be.

All the same, you feel quietly ashamed. You look at Biaojie and Biaomei, with the big personalities they have inherited from their mother and their blue satin dresses, already dirty, that can barely contain their spirited natures. You think that if they were in your shoes, they would thrive, they would not let a popular girl bother them, they would make lots of friends and Miss Cicely would adore them.

But here you are, the one given the opportunity,

and you are introverted, a dreamer, a wallflower. Somehow you will have to rise to the occasion even though you think it is impossible.

Think of your ancestors—they were farmers since the beginning of time, you hear Ma Ma say inside your head. You turn, and behind you stands the entirety of family that came before you, rooted into the ground. Breaking their backs under a merciless hot sun in an open rice field. *You, though, you will be a doctor. You will raise the status of our family name and bring honor in just one generation.* Ma Ma is telling you to be grateful and to run as far as you can from the hard life, but all you want to do is turn back and cry with the ghosts over their hopeless fates because yours feels just as wretched.

"Do you want to play?" asks Biaomei.

"I am much too old for childish games, but I will for the sake of both of you," says Biaojie, rolling her eyes.

Even though your other cousins are much older than you and they stand around pretending to be bored, the three of you fill the house with laughter and the Old Language, running up and down the stairs, giving Big Scary grief—until you think about Ba Ba and then you are quiet again. You wish Ma Ma would let you stay out of school while everyone is here. But at least you have the weekend, and that is enough in your heart to propel you forward.

That night Biaojie shares her comic books with you. You laugh at the pictures of a tall, lanky man called Old Master Q and his stumpy friend, Big Potato. The two sisters squish up on the queen mattress to make room, and the three of you lie in a row in the same Hello Ttkiy pajamas. They are made of thin cotton, suited to a warmer climate, so you pile First Uncle's crochet blankets on top and shiver deliciously under them. You think to yourself that before it even comes to pass, even though the specifics will be forgotten, this will be a memory you will always look back on with fondness.

"What are we going to do tomorrow?"

"Yeah, what are we going to do tomorrow? The olds are so boring!"

Biaojie turns the light off, and for some reason it is easier to talk in the dark. You feel brave enough to say it.

"I know somewhere that will amaze you both!"

Your cousins murmur between themselves. They are already unconvinced, already claiming disappointment.

"It's magic."

Biaojie howls in laughter and her little sister follows along to appear mature, even though you caught her checking the house earlier to make sure there weren't any monsters with wheels on the ends of their limbs like in the movie she saw on the plane.

"I'm serious," you say, feeling for your heart in the dark. Your cousins sense that they should listen.

"There is a magic house made of glass out back. Inside is a whole orange orchard. The sun and the moon somehow meet inside, even though they never meet in real life. There's also a pink serpent and a box of seeds that I will let you choose exactly one seed from. To begin with, anyway—you might have another if you visit again. Importantly, you can't go in unless the black-and-white gatekeeper says so first."

You think about mentioning First Uncle, but that might scare them, and also, they might laugh at you for believing in ghosts.

It is quiet. Then Biaojie calls you a liar. Biaomei is keen to support her sister, so she says it all sounds stupid. For a moment it stings, because it takes you back to school, but you push the pain aside and you laugh back at them. You're going to show them who is stupid.

It is quiet again. Biaojie says, "Fine," and then changes the topic. She declares that she is a big girl, so she is now interested in boys. It is you and Biaomei who make sounds of disgust this time, and you feel much better. Your cousin, a whole year older than you, then wants to know if *you* have a boyfriend and you reply, "Of course not!"

"Then why are you wearing a wedding ring?" Biaojie asks casually.

"It's on my middle finger," you point out.

Under the covers you twist Ah Ma's ring around. You wonder if boys who are friends are actually boy-friends. With that, your mind stirs up the mocking sounds of: "They are *lovers*" . . . "Both as dumb as each other!" . . . "Going to special class together!"

You push the sounds away with a yawn. Every-thing melts away until you are by yourself. A closet door opens and a neon pink light spills out, except you are only dreaming of yourself dreaming that you are back in your own room. Then the door shuts and it is dark.

CHAPTER FOURTEEN

Magpie

A magpie is warbling. Your eyes flicker open and you toss the blankets aside. Your cousins are entwined with each other and they yell for more sleep, but you march them out of bed. The rest of the house is asleep. Even Big Scary is still asleep, as there is not a single moan or creak. You feel the magic hanging in the air with the morning frost as the three of you descend the staircase, and you hush Biaojie for thumping so loudly with her big feet since anything might break the magic.

You think no one else will be up this early on a Saturday, but you are wrong. There is definitely a human eye looking through the hole in the fence. You march right up to it and press your own eye against it. A shocked Kevin falls backward on his side. You grin at the annoyed head that pops up over the fence. You want to tell Kevin that you were looking for him after school; that you wanted to show him something in that moment . . . and you still want to show him.

But you turn your head, seeking approval from your cousins. They have their arms folded and drawn inward, trying to appear hostile in their pink pajamas. Driven by group courage, you turn back to Kevin and engage in the longest exchange you've ever had with him.

"Why are you up so early? Are you looking for trouble?"

Kevin stares at you with an expression that says he hears that sort of comment all the time. "Why are *you* up so early? You must be looking for trouble too."

Now that the shoe is on the other foot, you feel insulted. You go to snarl at him, but you catch in his eye a look of hurt that you never saw before— perhaps because you've never purposely tried to be mean before, or even considered that he could be vulnerable—and you drop whatever comeback you had in your mouth.

"Do you want to see?" you say in a kinder voice, and you point at your cousins and then to the glass-house.

"What? That disgusting old thing? What could be interesting about that?"

Your chin lowers itself toward your chest without you being able to help yourself. You understand that he is only being mean because you were mean. That now you are locked in this spiral and it's hard to get out. You understand what it's like to be in his shoes. Kevin notices this change in you and his faces softens.

"Let's go look at the disgusting old thing, then. Maybe we'll find something cool. Like a nest of spiders."

Kevin pulls himself up to the top of the wooden fence and jumps over to your side, unafraid to land in the long grass. You didn't think he was capable of understanding that other people have feelings because he doesn't seem able to control his own. Maybe he is not who you think he is. It is so strange, but for that moment you believe you might be more than what you think you are.

Biaojie and Biaomei are both reluctant to leave the bottom step and go into the wild-looking backyard. They whisper to each other.

"What language are you two speaking?" Kevin says to them. "You need to speak the language that everyone speaks in this country."

You are not sure they fully understand what the strange boy from next door is saying, but you do and you feel embarrassed for everyone. Then it occurs to you that you've heard this sentiment being spoken before.

Outside the principal's office. At the punishment wall. The two teachers coming out of the faculty room. It appears Kevin has taken the message to heart and made it his own. You feel incredibly sad. You want to show him the glasshouse more than ever.

You want to show him how the glasshouse will help, heal, and protect him. That he is worth more than he considers himself. But you don't quite have the words to say it, so you think you will let the glasshouse tell it to him. You want to put your hand on his shoulder and ask him to stand next to you while you open the glasshouse door, but you are still wary all the time about what other people think of you.

So you march Biaojie and Biaomei up the flattened grass path while Kevin loiters in the yard pretending not to be interested. You see the black-and-white cat sleeping on top of a pile of old wooden crates. She acknowledges you with a stretch and a yawn. You nod in return.

Slowly turning the decrepit handle, the door of the glasshouse creaks open inch by inch. You all squeeze in, giggling because it feels as though you are doing something mischievous. You are busy trying to catch Kevin's reaction from behind you. Your cousins are pushing you forward, so you turn back around. And . . .

The glasshouse looks on the inside exactly how it looks on the outside.

There's just a jumble of old gardening equipment, a tower of empty plastic pots, and when something in the corner rattles, you all scream.

You stare at the situation in dismay. A pot falls over and dirt spills out.

"Is this the orange orchard?" Biaojie points to a skinny plant in a pot that has turned brown and died due to neglect.

"And is this what you meant by the sun and the moon?" teases Biaomei, pulling on a rusty wind chime that depicts the solar system. At her touch the metal moon falls off and rolls under some junk. From the middle of the junk pile comes a loud hissing noise.

"Well, that is obviously the pink serpent," scoffs Biaojie, tossing a rake aside and moving a rusty old lawn mower out of the way. The hissing sounds again, and your older cousin bends over to take a look into the gap.

That is when the very real pink serpent slithers out at lightning-fast speed and, with more scream-ing, you retreat just as fast out of the glasshouse and toward the back steps.

"You *are* a liar!" is the first thing that Biaojie says. She is happy that she was right.

"That was scary, it wasn't fun at all," says Biaomei, looking teary.

Had it been a dream? Your imagination? Something worse? But you know it's real because you still remember the feel of your blue wisteria, the knotted wood of the trunk against your back. The smell of orange blossoms and fresh soil in the air. The sun's magical rays on your skin. You stare back at the glasshouse with a sense of embarrassment. And disappointment, but mostly betrayal. You greeted the gatekeeper. You did everything right.

Your cousins stand awkwardly in silence before an "Ahh!" comes from Biaojie.

"It was all a joke, wasn't it? Well, I admit it—you fooled us good!"

Biaojie starts to laugh loudly, even though there is no joy in her voice and the laugh she does manage to push out sounds like a hollow echo. Her little sister joins in. Then the two of them are up and away, racing and mounting the steps two at a time, and although they are only going back into the house, it feels as though they are leaving you behind. They have each other. You have nobody.

"That was the lamest thing ever," says Kevin, and

he makes his way to the fence and climbs back over to his side. You are now truly alone.

"Why didn't you show your true self?"

The glasshouse doesn't reply.

A pair of crows fighting atop one of the domed arches fly off in vocal anger and leave poop on the glass.

You refuse to look at the glasshouse anymore out of disgust. You search for the black-and-white cat, but she is nowhere to be seen, the pile of wooden crates unoccupied. You plead for Big Scary to show you a sign, so that you know that at least someone cares about you. She gives nothing back to you but the façade of a house. You are alone and confused again.

Ma Ma is awake and in the kitchen. A new urn sits on the stovetop, boiling gallons of water at once so that lots of instant coffee can be pumped out at the same time. Ma Ma has a smile on her face. You have not known her to be willingly awake this early or be so happy about it.

First, Second, and Fourth Aunty sit around the kitchen table, idly chatting and taking turns scraping one another's backs with a wooden back scratcher. They all smell like the Kwan Loong oil that they have been furiously rubbing onto their throats and inside their nostrils in a bid to ward off the cold weather.

You imagine the lot of them sitting in the ancestral home in the Old Land, with the huge ancestral altar in the front room, thick with incense and the ghosts of grandparents and the past. You think about offerings made on the altar in the form of oranges, oil, and fresh flowers. About how you have to clasp your hands together and give respect to the framed photo of Ah Ma and Ah Gong, so they will in turn give blessings to you.

Mrs. Huynh is also seated at the table, and she looks mighty uncomfortable. Ma Ma is making no effort to talk to her as Ma Ma is too busy being the center of attention.

"You need to buy a hallway table and make a small shrine for him," says First Aunty, referring to Ba Ba.

"I've decided against the idea," replies Ma Ma. "I don't want to follow the old traditions here."

Second Aunty gasps at this response and gives the corners of her own mouth small smacks even though it wasn't her who said it.

"This is a nice, clean, modern house and I don't want incense ash everywhere and a blackened ceiling from all the smoke," says Ma Ma. She passes cups of coffee around.

First Aunty snorts loudly and starts hacking up

imaginary phlegm, and Mrs. Huynh leans right back. In your mind you believe that Mrs. Huynh's Old Land and your aunt's home mustn't be that far separated, so she should be used to this type of behavior. Maybe Mrs. Huynh has been in the New Land for too long.

All you know is that Mrs. Huynh looks at the pile of frozen chicken wings defrosting in the sink, the stack of old newspapers that will become tonight's tablecloth, everything accommodated for, and she excuses herself politely to go home.

"We saw a pink serpent." Biaomei tugs on the arm of her mother.

"What did I tell you about not going out back? It's a jungle. I wouldn't be surprised if you got eaten by a tiger."

"But Meixing never said anything about tigers, only a pink serpent, orange trees, and the sun and the moon both at the same time."

Fourth Aunty gives you a long look. It's not an encouraging one.

"You need to quell your daughter's imagination," your aunt says to Ma Ma, as if you were invisible. "Thinking too much along those lines is not good for the brain. I suppose the discipline at the schools here is quite lenient."

You hide another piece of yourself on the inside.

You will not speak unless you are spoken to.

Second Aunty is flipping through an old photo album—you are not sure where she got it. Maybe Big Scary has revealed another secret cupboard. She points to the picture of the Sad Bride, the same one in the framed photo on the formal dining room wall.

"That is Ah Ma on her wedding day. An arranged marriage. Back in the day when women didn't have many prospects."

You twist the ring on your finger in a shared sorrow.

CHAPTER FIFTEEN

Moth

Monday comes and it is the dreaded day. You think about the white shirt and black pants Ma Ma has arranged for you to wear this evening; she says you must dress in the colors of a magpie. You are haunted by the vision of the shirt and pants, spread out on the bed, looking as though whoever had been wearing them had lain down and then disappeared.

A big fuss is made about what lunch you should take to school because each of your aunts wants to be the one to prepare it. First Aunty wins, as she always does because she is the oldest, and she makes you a freshly cooked, three-course meal in a three-level tiffin box. She even offers to come to you at lunchtime and spoon-feed you. You respectfully decline this in horror.

On the way out you see Mrs. Huynh standing at

her mailbox, but she isn't taking any letters out. She stares at you sadly, perhaps hoping you will make eye contact and tell her something about Ma Ma. You come so close to telling her that you miss her and maybe Ma Ma misses her too and she should come over. But you can't put this into words, and it has nothing to do with language barriers.

You concentrate on getting through the day, through class, so you can go home again. The reward of playing with your cousins means you have to do your work, stay out of trouble, keep quiet, lie low. Until Miss Cicely taps you on the shoulder and asks to speak to you privately outside.

"One of your classmates has accused you of stealing from them."

You look at Miss Cicely, confused.

"She says that you took a gold ring that belonged to her. Do you know what she's talking about?"

Your mouth opens. Then it closes. You both stare down at the band on your finger. You shake your head furiously.

"It's a very serious allegation, Meixing, do you understand? Maybe you didn't mean to take it on purpose. You can tell me the truth."

You don't feel surprised even though it stings, having no idea how to begin explaining. If you try to say it was *her* who stole *your* ring, it will sound like *you* are lying. What a mess! Your mind is running so fast that if you try to speak the words they will only trip over your tongue and fall out in a confused heap.

"Meixing. This is simply unacceptable." Miss Cicely's pretty face becomes scrunched. "We have tried our very best to accommodate you, even sending you to a special learning class. We've welcomed you into this country, and you repay this by—"

Miss Cicely seems to realize what she is saying and stops, but it is too late. You have lost confidence in her ability to believe whatever truth you might tell her. Your heart sinks and you have never felt so worthless in your entire life.

For the second time your ring is taken from you. And maybe it should hurt less the second time because you never expected to get the ring back the first time. But maybe it hurts more because this time someone you should be able to trust has taken it.

You sit as heavy as a stone for the rest of the school day, feeling as though you are going to break through the seat of your chair. Hands weighted, eyelids down. Somewhere in the pit of your stomach Ah Ma's ring swishes and sloshes uneasily in the souring juices.

To your disappointment, there is no playing with your cousins when you get home. You are told to change and then rushed straight out the door again.

The service is held at a small funeral parlor. All is quiet in the room, where there's a worship table covered in a red cloth. The Buddhist priest, the laypeople dressed in their traditional robes, and your relatives all arrive. The funeral ladies in their neat pencil skirts and matching blazers stand at the doorway and stare. But Ailing has paid for everything, so they keep their curiosity politely to themselves.

You see the shiny brown coffin in the corner of the room, covered in flowers, and a portrait of your father when he was young, stiff and serious, perhaps taken after high school at a professional photo place. Why this photo? You don't know. He doesn't even look like that anymore. You try not to look. It feels unreal because under that lid, you think to yourself, anyone could be in there.

You still expect Ba Ba to come home and say it's all been a mistake, that he just needed more time to get over the argument he had with Ma Ma. Wasn't it all a funny misunderstanding? He learned his lesson, he's never going to hurt either of you again, and he is going to the store right now to buy you that plastic pony.

Imagine if the lid opened to reveal a magician's box, with a velvet lining adorned with silver stars inside, and Ba Ba steps out to take a bow?

But the coffin stays shut and silent.

Everyone is dressed in the same white shirts and black pants as you. You think of magpies and you wonder what they are grieving for in their funeral feathers. In your mind you remember a fairy tale Ma Ma once told you about a boy and a girl at the opposite ends of the Milky Way and how all the magpies made a bridge to connect them. Perhaps the magpies are sad that they can help the couple meet only once a year.

One of your older, responsible girl cousins is in charge of handing out the white lengths of cloth for everyone to tie around their heads. Even though everyone is supposed to be mourning, your boy cousins start laughing and making Karate Kid moves at each other before their mothers threaten to cane them.

You want to stay with Biaojie and Biaomei, but you have to go up front with Ma Ma as an immediate family member. She wears a red scarf around her neck to protect the life inside of her because no ghost or bad spirit can get through such a powerful, happy color. Each of your Aunties and the priest have advised Ma Ma against being part of the actual ceremony, as she is so humongous and because it is plain bad luck, but Ma Ma would not be persuaded. Cultures and superstitions and rituals are so hard to understand, you think, especially since they can be chopped and changed at any given moment.

You all kneel down in the room, and the service starts.

The priest chants and a lot of incense is lit and everyone has to stand up and kneel down and stand up and walk around in circles and kneel down again. You are worried about Ma Ma and her huge tummy as her face turns red from the struggle, but she bats your hand away and you put it behind your back so that it won't try doing that again.

Ailing, so highly foreign educated but completely ignorant about the proceedings of a traditional funeral, comes up front to try to solve the problem. She is sharply told to go back in place.

Your eyes water, not because you are crying— you don't truly believe Ba Ba is gone—but from the fragrant smoke wafting around. Bells are rung, fingers are formed into prayer hands, and foreheads are touched to the ground. The funeral parlor ladies stand politely by the door and try to keep their eyes from bulging and their mouths from commenting.

As you stand up once again, your legs and knees become very sore and you wonder what this is truly for, but it is something that has been done for generations so it's something that has to be done today.

At one point you look up and see, at the back of the room, where an empty row of chairs is set up for observers, Mrs. Huynh and Kevin sitting there silently. Kevin is wearing a suit and his hair has been flattened down into a shiny black wing. The ceremony continues and time seems to go on forever. Tears are streaming down your face, but you are not crying.

As you kneel on the floor staring blankly, the only sounds being the priest's chants and a ringing bell, a large brown moth flutters in from the darkness outside and lands on the wall. It stays there for the whole rest of the proceeding, occasionally lifting its furry wings.

"It's your father!" Biaojie whispers into your ear, as you all complete another circle around the room. "He's come to watch."

You don't know whether to believe her.

After the ceremony is over, a red packet is shoved into your hand. When you look inside, there is a coin for good luck and a wrapped sweet to take away the bitter taste of death. You put the coin in your pocket and eat the sweet. You look over to where Kevin and his mother were sitting, but they have vanished.

Tired and drained, you all pile into the taxis waiting outside and go back home, except Ma Ma and Ailing, who need to finalize what remains to be done. You want to stay behind too because Ba Ba might still reveal his secret magic trick at the last minute, but you are told by Ma Ma that you have no part in adult business.

Big Scary is waiting for you to get back with every single light on. Which is strange since, when you left, it wasn't dark yet and nobody had turned on any lights. Everyone swears it wasn't them playing a prank, but they laugh anyway due to nerves. The taxi drivers are not superstitious; they want the hesitant passengers to get out so they can get paid.

Everyone stands at the bottom of the steps and looks upward.

"I think this house is haunted," says Fifth Aunty.

"I didn't want to be the first to say it," replies Fourth Aunty in the whispered tone she keeps for gossip. "The house seems to get bigger every single day. This morning I swear I found an extra bathroom."

"I don't think it's a harmful spirit," agrees Fifth Aunty. "I personally wouldn't mind having a house that got bigger."

"Too much cleaning," chimes in Third Aunty in all seriousness.

"Still, I think a Taoist master should be invited in to clean it out."

You look up at Big Scary and wonder why it is so necessary to get rid of anything that is considered weird or different. Big Scary pulses that secret code—three short signals, followed by three long signals, and then the three short signals again—that you have seen her do once before. No one else sees. But you understand, and in the dark you hold your open palm up toward her as a sign that you stand with her.

"I know what's going to happen," Biaojie whispers into your ear. "On the seventh day Ba Ba's ghost will come home, thinking that he is still alive. Everyone has to stay up to keep vigil, and when he sees everyone, he will realize he is dead and will know he has to go to the other side."

The other side of what, she doesn't say.

You're not sure how much to believe of what Biaojie tells you—after all, she is only one year older than you—but she has the ease and confidence to talk to any child or adult and find out such things. You envy her. It is true that everyone is staying until the end of the week, so maybe your cousin is right.

"Have you ever seen a ghost?" she asks.

You think about First Uncle and how you spoke to him not that long ago, but you say nothing.

"Neither have I, but I'm hoping to get scared!"

You think about ghosts and you are no longer scared by them. Since you came to this New Land, you are no longer a child who is scared of monsters or fox spirits or rotting, hopping vampires. You stand against the dark and your heart is calm and big. You know what you are scared of in this world and that is people and their expectations and hatred and unkindness.

You look up. Inside the Room on the Roof, the eye opens, neon purple against the black sky. It sees you and then closes again.

During the following week, while everyone waits for Ba Ba to show up, all your relatives pile into the rented van and Ailing drives them around sightseeing and shopping. There are certain things that all the adults want: massive bottles of fish oil capsules, massive tubs of moisturizing cream, and chocolate. Lots of chocolate, blocks and boxes of it, which they cram into their suitcases and which you are afraid will melt and stick together into a giant lump in the humid atmosphere back in the Old Land.

The kids, on the other hand, want to pet the animals at the wildlife park, go to the beach, and find out if black swans are real. Biaojie and Biaomei regale you with their adventure stories while you, unfortunately, have to go to school. You can't wait for the weekend so you can jump in the van too.

When Saturday finally arrives, Ailing drives everyone to the wharf and it rains all the way there. Huddled under the sheltered part of the boardwalk, eating the world-famous fish-and-chips off soggy paper, you stare at the choppy grey water. Your aunts complain about the price of everything even though they don't pay for it. Your older cousins take photos of each other with a disposable camera that will turn out blurry and dark when they are developed. Everyone shuffles back to the van. It rains all the way back too. You are thrilled by every second of it.

Ma Ma is happy for Ailing to be the tour guide, and she stays home with First Aunty, who keeps her company and brews her different nourishing herbal soups and remedies. You have never seen her happier, her eyes shining above a steaming bowl, as First Aunty does all the talking and she quietly sips. You quietly despise her for not crying about Ba Ba anymore, because you still do.

Ma Ma's great big metal steamer is constantly hissing in the kitchen. She makes trays of *kueh* in all colors: seven-layer *kueh* in pink, yellow, and white; sweet blue rice with a layer of *pandan*—green custard—on top; red tortoises the size of your hand that open up to reveal yellow bean paste. She tries to teach Ailing, but Ailing is not very good at it and Ma Ma says it's because she has lost her heritage.

Ma Ma even goes as far outside as the back steps of Big Scary and looks at the backyard, musing about growing long beans and bitter melons. You remember how the three of you as a family used to plant the same things in the communal vegetable patch back home. Ma Ma has clearly forgotten, as she does not make any mention of it. In your heart a kernel of resentment lodges and grows.

The week passes, and it is time for Ba Ba to come home.

CHAPTER SIXTEEN

Cocoon

O n the seventh night after the funeral there is a different sort of energy in the house— so charged, you can almost see the atmosphere crackle and pop, although no one says a thing. It's as though everyone is waiting for something to happen, although no one knows quite what.

You are all gathered in the living room. The living room has never had this much space; Big Scary has made it so everyone can fit. The adults play a card game called "bridge" while your older cousins teach you, Biaojie, and Biaomei various games that have slightly different rules but are all called "fish."

It is hard to stay focused, and at times the others think you are forgetful or purposely trying to cheat, but you are nodding off because it has been hard for you to sleep.

Ever since Biaojie told you that large brown moth

was your father, you have been looking for him not only in your waking life, but also while you sleep. He always eludes you, always just beyond reach, hiding in the fuzzy corners of your dreams and imagination. You look under the orange shade above the coffee table, thinking you see shadows, but there is only a bare bulb. You clasp the lucky coin from the funeral in your palm.

It is nearing midnight and nobody says a thing.

Not even Ma Ma to tell you that it's a school night and you should go to bed.

Until Third Aunty, with a giant yawn and a stretching of the arms that makes everyone jump, declares that she is falling asleep and is turning in. Everyone watches in silence as she shuffles toward the staircase. You all hear the creaky sounds of wood echoing upward. Everyone huddles a little closer.

There is a wind blowing that is making a mysterious howling sound as it enters the house through a gap that no one can locate. First Aunty decides that this is the best time to start telling a ghost story.

"On the night of your Ah Gong's homecoming," she says to the group of cousins huddled in front of her, "we were all gathered like we are now. It was seven days after your grandfather's funeral. Biaoge was only a toddler and he was asleep in a different room in his cot."

All eyes turn to First Aunty's eldest son. He acts cool, but the tips of his ears have already turned red. This is obviously not the first time his mother has told the story.

"At the stroke of midnight we suddenly heard a wail coming from Biaoge's bedroom, so I raced there to see him standing upright in the dark, holding on to the wooden bars of his cot. I asked him what was the matter, and do you know what he told me?"

The cousins hold their breath and shake their heads.

"He told me that Ah Gong had come into his room and taken away his pacifier."

The cousins scream.

You wish that you could scream too. But everyone else's nightmares have become your dreams. You want Ba Ba to show himself. You won't be scared. You will embrace him.

"You don't remember it, do you, Biaoge?"

He shakes his head and his cheeks burn.

"They say that children can see ghosts, but we lose the ability once we grow up and stop believing in magic and the supernatural. The curious thing is that we searched everywhere, but we never did find that pacifier."

At that precise moment the clock on the kitchen

wall ticks over to midnight. First Aunty stops talking. No one says a thing. You have no idea what is going to happen.

Nothing happens.

You all wait a little longer.

Still nothing happens.

Eventually, it seems pointless to sit around anymore and you all start drifting off in different directions to brush teeth, clean faces, and change into nightclothes. You sit in your pink bed, empty and teary, staring out the window, the coin grasped tightly in your hand. Every time you squeeze it, you think you can hear a ringing inside your head. You think of the priest's bell at the funeral, the crystal notes echoing out, guiding Ba Ba's soul. You squeeze the coin again and you ask Ba Ba to be with you.

You believe in magic and the supernatural and you will never stop believing. You want Ba Ba to come home. You place your hand on the windowpane. Instead of feeling cold, it feels warm to the touch.

That is when you notice that in the top corner of the window frame a little pink caterpillar is perched upside down on the wood.

"Ba Ba?" you whisper, standing up on your mattress to take a better look.

The caterpillar is spinning a soft pink cocoon, and you watch it weave its magic around itself as you try to keep your tired eyes open. Outside, the glass-house is silent and dark. But inside your bedroom, the wardrobe door creaks open and pink light spills out. A hazy smoke billows and covers the entire floor, and you feel that you might be floating on a bed with no legs, suspended in the air and in time.

A moment later you find yourself floating down the stairs of Big Scary in a funny haze between half awake and almost asleep to stand in the doorway of the kitchen. You are now wide awake.

Standing over the stovetop in front of a crackling frying pan is Ailing, wearing an oversized white sleeping shirt with CHOOSE LIFE written in big block letters. The black-and-white cat is crouched on the floor, eating sardines off a dinner plate.

"Want some scrambled eggs?" she says, holding two eggs out to you.

You take them and crack them into her bowl. Ailing beats them with a fork and pours the mixture into the pan, handing you a wooden spoon.

"Can't sleep either?"

You shake your head.

"I remember the day your Ah Gong died clearly. I went to the funeral, but I wasn't considered one of his daughters so I wasn't allowed to participate in any of the rituals," says Ailing, picking the empty plate off the ground. "I could only watch as a guest."

Ailing shows you how to stir the eggs properly so they become soft yellow clouds.

"I felt a twin sort of sadness for a long time. Sadness over the actual loss and also sadness that I wasn't allowed to grieve properly."

You look at Ailing. It is bad luck to talk about funerals and people who have died, your Aunties all say so. You have to keep it respectfully on the inside. But you are glad Ailing is talking about it because you know exactly what she means; the understanding goes right down to your bones.

"If you ever feel like you need someone to talk to, you call me when I get home, okay? I'll write down my phone number for you—it's really long."

You feel a bit better about this. It doesn't take the pain away, but the square of paper she gives you is like a little life raft.

As you both eat your late-night meal in the living room, you look under the orange shade again and the bulb under it is glowing pink. Ailing doesn't seem to notice. You don't know if you are awake anymore. Suddenly, you are tired.

Sometime in the middle of the night you wake

to find yourself back in bed and the blanket pulled over you, although you don't remember going back to bed and you don't remember tucking yourself in. The caterpillar has finished spinning its cocoon, which hangs in the corner of the window like a tiny ball of cotton candy. You feel a sense of hope that Ba Ba has come home.

CHAPTER SEVENTEEN

Suitcases

Morning has come and everyone is leaving. Everything is happening the same as the first day, but in reverse. Things are going back into suitcases. Rooms are emptying out. Biaojie and Biaomei are once again dressed in their best outfits for the plane trip home, tucking hard candies into pockets instead of throwing empty wrappers out. Time is now going to take everything back until the last door is closed and everyone is gone.

You can feel Big Scary packing herself up too; bathrooms and bedrooms are already disappearing, and you are powerless to stop it, even as you try your hardest to get ready for school. The secret staircase is still secret, so you quietly slip downstairs before it becomes a wall.

Ma Ma is in her bedroom again, her shoulder and head drawn down toward her belly, as if she intends to disappear into herself. First Aunty has her hand on Ma Ma's shoulder and is consoling her, but all Ma Ma does is shake her head to everything.

"Now remember that you will have to go to the temple every seven days and have the monks say a prayer for the next forty-nine days," says First Aunty. "You want him to be reborn into a better life, don't you?"

"Can you not stay any longer, Jie Jie?"

It's First Aunty's turn to shake her head.

Ma Ma puts her face in her hands.

You can't bear to watch this scene because it is just a different sort of grieving playing out, so you run out the front door.

There, in the early-morning light just after dawn, you find Ailing sitting on the top of the stone steps, reading a thick novel. She goes to shut the book when she hears you, a guilty look on her face, but then she stops.

"Sorry, automatic reflex. I used to secretly stay up and read books by flashlight, way past my bedtime. Guess I'm still scared of getting into trouble."

All you've ever heard are the stories of how spoiled and undisciplined Ailing was as a child, so this comes as a bit of a surprise to you.

Making sure nothing in the universe is disturbed,

you sit down so gently and calmly that she looks down at the page she's currently on and decides to leave the book open. You stare at the tiny letters and the tissue-thin paper.

"One day you'll be able to read books like this too, I promise," says Ailing.

You feel incredibly sad to have to correct her, but then you think of what the glasshouse showed you. The promise touches your face softly and wraps itself gently around you, planting a seed of hope in your heart.

"Tell me, do you like it here?" asks Ailing. "Do you like school?"

You wish you could tell Ailing the truth. That you don't look forward to going to school every morning, that you feel a terrible lump in your stomach when you have to leave the house. That you don't mind it so much when you get there, but you don't ever feel safe, except in Ms. Jardine's class. You feel that something horrible is going to happen, all the time.

Instead, you tuck your hands between your legs and you tell her you wish you weren't so different.

Ailing smiles at you, and she takes the hand that you release and squeezes it.

"You're going to be okay, Meixing. Your world will slowly change, but I can't guarantee that you won't always feel different. But, you know, it's not so bad to be a misfit."

She makes a strange snorting noise and sighs. Ailing is a curious being. She has no formal title in a family where you are expected to call everyone by one. You even have to call all your cousins by their titles, though it would be easier to use their real names. But Ailing is just Ailing. A stranger. A nobody. Everyone accepts her help and her money, but although she shares the same blood, she will never be accepted as family.

"Well, for what it's worth, I really like it here. It's quiet, I can hear myself think." Ailing sighs wistfully. "Maybe I might even move here one day. For some strange reason it feels like . . . home."

You look at Ailing and there are stars and dreams in her eyes.

"I could buy myself a house, not too big or too small, just enough for one person, and it could be close by to where you are now! You could come over and hang out. Actually, do! You must come and see how many books I have! We can drink milky tea and I could bake a cake—although I am terrible at desserts, as everyone knows."

Your whole being sighs with her.

"Or we can stay up past midnight and cook scrambled eggs!" Ailing winks at you.

So it wasn't a dream after all.

But the little quiet bubble you both inhabit suddenly bursts. Your aunts and cousins, suitcases and boxes, all spill out of the house and tumble down the stone steps toward the van. Ailing gets up, stretches, and leans over to pull a large green leaf from a nearby magnolia tree. She tucks it into her book and finally closes it.

Ma Ma is the last to come out. She stands one step past the doorframe. Her face is pinched tightly and only a few expressions away from bursting into tears.

"Thank you for letting us all stay, Ping. It has been good to see you again." Ailing calls your mother by her real name. She doesn't mention the funeral.

"Come and visit again, Ailing," your mother replies. She doesn't mention the funeral either.

For a moment you think Ailing is going to lean forward and embrace your mother with a full-hearted hug, but having made that mistake once already, she stays where she is and your mother stays where she is.

"Goodbye . . ." Ailing turns to go and then adds as an afterthought, "Jie Jie."

"Goodbye," Ma Ma replies, and that is it. She does not call Ailing her Mei Mei, her "little sister." Ailing looks quietly devastated. She hurries down the stone steps as fast as she can and into the van, every-one already packed and waiting for her. Maybe she's running so that she can make it into the driver's seat before the tears pour out.

For Ailing, your heart grows and then it shrinks again, as it is apt to do when you receive love and then that love gets taken away from you. You watch as the van with all the people who matter to you drives away down the road, then turns around the corner, out of sight and out of your lives.

Then you think about the last time someone you loved drove away from you. They never came back.

CHAPTER EIGHTEEN

Backpack

M a Ma's eyes are empty like the hallways of Big Scary. She blinks and then hurries quickly back into the house, a chill seeming to take over her. Her footsteps echo deep and hollow. You don't know what to do with your loss. If your heart is now so empty, why does it feel so heavy? Then you wonder why you grieve everyone leaving more than the loss of your father, and you feel like less of a daughter.

The morning light makes you sad; the empty space that Ailing took up reading her novel makes you ache, so you go back inside, following your mother's ghostly tracks. The hallway of the house has shrunk. The staircase feels narrower. You remember how Biaojie and Biaomei ran down it side by side as you chased after them, but now as you go up, the railings squeeze in against your elbows.

Your room feels so much smaller. Even your bed feels smaller. The bathroom you have been using for the past week has disappeared. As you walk past, all you find is a wall. The room that Biaojie and Biaomei were sharing, and asked you once to share with them, is gone.

It's as if the house is contracting itself in the same way you are: withdrawing.

Sitting on your bed, though, is something pink and glowing. Curiously, you approach. It is a brand-new backpack. You unzip the top and inside is a new pencil case and new school supplies to replace the old ones that Mrs. Huynh had kindly cobbled together for you. On the floor is a new pair of white sneakers. With rainbow shoelaces.

You hug the whole lot. You want to tumble back into bed and fall asleep with them in your arms. You suspect it is the doing of Ailing, and you wonder why she didn't give the gifts to you in person so you could thank her properly. But she is already gone.

Happily, you transfer the contents of your burlap bag to your new backpack. You take out the activity sheets that you have completed for Ms. Jardine, and they make you smile. You don't care that they are for meant for younger kids. You touch the shiny stickers on them. They say things like GOOD TRY! and KEEP UP

THE GREAT WORK! There is one with an airplane on it that says YOU'RE ALMOST THERE! You don't always get everything perfect, but Ms. Jardine makes you want to try your best.

You like to carry the worksheets around even though you can keep them in a drawer at home. They give you hope.

The wide padded straps of the shiny new backpack feel good. You stand entirely taller, prouder, with your shoulders pulled back. You decide that you are going to keep wearing your boys' shoes because they have got to the stage where they are now soft and comfortable. Although you hated them at first, you have grown to like them. Just as you have grown to like Big Scary. You put the new white sneakers into the wardrobe.

Before you leave the room, you stand on your bed and get your face as close as you can to the pink cocoon. You tell Ba Ba you miss him, and you take your coin sitting on the windowsill and press it in your palm. Somewhere in the distance a bell rings out. You drop the coin in your pocket. *Be here with me,* you silently say. The cocoon trembles gently.

You go back downstairs. Ma Ma is curled up on her side in her bed, staring at the wall.

So you pack your own lunch, making yourself

a sandwich with the chicken slices that Ailing left behind. You also take one of her snack-sized yogurts. You will ask Ma Ma or Mrs. Huynh if they can keep buying these things.

Because there are leftover chicken wings, you take a small portion of them too. Yes, you are going to eat them with your fingers, because you know that no matter what you do or do not do, it's never going to be right.

There will always be something else about you to pick on.

So you might as well be yourself.

"Her bag makes it seem like she's trying to be part of the cool kids," you hear your former friend whisper to the others as you sit down at your desk when you get to school that morning.

"And those shoes! Her parents must have spent all their money on the bag and are too broke to afford decent shoes!"

It hurts. Especially the bit about your parents, without knowing anything about your family, but you tell yourself not to care. You don't want her fake type of friendship anyway, especially when Ah Ma's ring is now back on her finger. Thank goodness you found out what she was really like, even though you learned the hard way. You want to become a real and true version of yourself, like Ailing and the glasshouse think you can.

You find out something new and extraordinary about Kevin when you go to the rickety old portable class-room with the fossilized mulch pile. He can draw. After a whole week of back-and-forth Ms. Jardine has finally convinced him to give it a go. He starts the task of illustrating the page of text that Ms. Jardine gave him on the first day, and you stare in amaze-ment at the weird creatures and humanoid figures that spill out onto the page. Monsters with one eye, two eyes, fifty-three eyes under a very long eyelid.

Josh has a good look at them and then he offers a high five to Kevin. Kevin smacks his palm back with so much enthusiasm that Josh shakes his hand afterward in pain. Kevin boasts that his drawings are much better than Josh's and that he's going to be a famous artist when he grows up. Ms. Jardine tells him that everyone can be good in their own way. Then he points to one of your sketches and says that it is "crap." Ms. Jardine tells him not to use that word and to apologize, but he doesn't.

You are exasperated by him. But then you think about what Ms. Jardine would do. She would never give up on Kevin, and you decide you won't either.

You know hardly anything about him and, like you, he could be acting this way because he's not so happy. You think about the word Ailing used—"misfit." Somehow the word makes you belong. You and Kevin and Josh are just three people who don't quite fit in, but why should you have to? Your heart grows.

"At the end of the term," says Ms. Jardine, "we are going to have a party of sorts. I'm going to bring some sweets and invite your families. You will all present your creations on a little stage I'm going to make and read them out loud."

You wonder if Ms. Jardine is going to address the invitation to both Ma Ma and Ba Ba. You want to tell her she doesn't have to worry about inviting Ba Ba, and you start to tremble. You reach into your pocket to hold on to the coin, and it helps with the shakes.

"I won't be able to do it," growls Kevin, throwing his colored pencil down. "I'm too stupid."

You secretly feel the same way. You look down at the story you are creating and you feel shy and anxious that your voice will retreat and that this time it won't come back.

"Don't ever say that about yourself," replies Ms. Jardine. "Look, if someone took me to a completely foreign country today and threw me out onto the street, how do you think I'd do trying to speak the language and understand the customs?"

"You'd be okay. You're an adult," Kevin points out.

"I reckon I'd starve to death! That's if I didn't get thrown in jail first for my unorthodox views!" Ms. Jardine laughs. "I'm confident that all of you will ace the end-of-term assignments. None of you are 'stupid'— look at what you've created so far. I couldn't be more proud."

Ms. Jardine always makes everything better. But when you close your eyes, you see an empty chair in the audience in front of you where your mother should be.

There is a tap on your shoulder, and Josh shows you the olive tree he is drawing.

"I was too scared before to draw anything from my old home. I didn't think anyone would be interested anyway. But now I think it's important. Thank you." Josh takes something out of his backpack and slides it in front of you. It is a jar of home-preserved olives.

"These are from my mom. They are delicious, although if you haven't grown up eating them, they might taste strange at first. But they are much better than raw!"

"Thank you," you whisper.

"This is just a small sample. We preserve them in huge bottles at home, so if you grow fond of them, I can give you one of those!"

You smile. It takes both your hands to lift up the jar. You wonder about the size of the huge bottles.

Then Kevin spoils the moment by grabbing the jar away from you and giving it a violent shake.

"Yuck," he says loudly. "What is this foreign food?"

Ms. Jardine asks him to give it back to you and not to say what he said again. She tries asking Josh to explain about the olives, asking you what you think of them, but Kevin marches off into a corner, folds his arms, and refuses to listen. You do get the jar back, though.

Ms. Jardine talks to him quietly and convinces him to come sit back down.

Kevin is in too much of a mood to walk with you back to class, so you walk with Josh instead while Kevin skulks in the background and follows. You carry your jar of olives close to your chest, and you both stop at the undercover assembly area to look at a production an older class is working on.

There are some kids up on the raised concrete area that serves as a stage. They are practicing their parts, dressed as a princess and a knight in love, and there's a moon whose only role is to become a crescent and turn back to a full moon again, behind all the drama at the forefront. There are two poor kids who play the front and the back ends of the same horse.

Others are busy painting and making backdrops.

Then there is one kid holding an all-too-familiar yellow flyer. He's trying to show it to his classmates.

"Look what my big brother gave me! He says I can join his gang once I'm older. He's going to get me a pair of combat boots just like his."

Most of them ignore him. Others wrinkle up their faces. Some of them laugh. You grab Josh's arm as a warning that you should leave. But it is too late, the boy on stage has already seen you both.

"See this? I think this is you." He walks right up to you and holds the leaflet to your face so that it touches your nose. You look away and refuse to engage. This big kid is a whole head taller than you. Your heart is beating blood into your ears and you want to get away. But here you are, frozen to the spot.

"Leave her alone," Josh manages to mumble. The kid calls Josh something you don't understand, but it makes Josh's face open up like a wound. The kid leaves and you both start walking away, as calmly as you can. But then he comes back with a friend. The friend grins and aims a water pistol at Josh's face. Josh has no other option but to stand there and let the water hit his glasses.

That's when you decide to drop the jar of olives. It lands on the first kid's foot with a satisfying thud, and it must have hurt, as he's jumping around and swearing. This draws everyone's attention. Now you're in big trouble. The cracked jar rolls off. There are olives all over the ground. You don't think you can run; you don't think you can scream, either. The boy moves a little closer. You prepare to learn a lesson you don't think is fair and shut your eyes.

Until someone comes flying toward the bully, and suddenly there is a fight going on. It's Kevin. You had forgotten about Kevin. He's younger than the other kid, but since he's also a whole head taller than you, he's giving it a really good go. Everyone else is yelling or watching stunned, but someone has the good sense to call for a teacher.

After the last school bell has rung for the day, you see Kevin back at the strangely cheerful punishment wall, this time with an impressive bruise on his face. You press yourself against the wall next to him.

"You didn't have to do that," you say to him.

"Are you trying to say that you're a girl who doesn't need a boy to protect her?" Kevin yells at you. "Well, I was only trying to help a *friend*. That is all!"

"Thank you. You are my friend too," you say.

Kevin has opened his mouth, ready to shout something else, before he realizes what you have said.

"You called me a friend first," you point out.

"Yeah," he says, and his jaw relaxes so much that the rest of the sentence becomes a set of mumbles. You think he is suggesting that you both take off and leave the school behind. It is exactly how you feel, but instead you say to him:

"You cannot run away from your problems." You look at him clearly in the eye. "You must stay and learn and *win*."

He seems to comprehend what you are trying to say, and the anger in his eyes flickers a little less angrily.

The door to the principal's office opens, and the kid Kevin fought comes out. He sees the two of you and makes a symbol with his hand and walks off. It is Kevin's turn to go inside. You don't know if the principal is a good or a bad guy; on your side or not on your side. These days your whole world has been clearly split into two.

CHAPTER NINETEEN

Medicine

Y ou and Josh wait for Kevin at the utility pole. You tell Josh that you are sorry about the jar of olives. He jokingly tells you not to worry because his mother has five hundred more jars at home. You feel that in saying so, he is suggesting that it is friendship that is not so easily replaceable. Josh is nervous and ill at ease with himself as he picks at the little bits of yellow paper on the pole with his thumbnail. You both shiver against the cold that has never felt so bitter.

You see him first, that figure hunched against the world with his hands in his pockets. You want to know what the principal said to him, eager to know if everything is all right, but he is reluctant to talk. You tell him that there is a place he needs to be right now. You say "please."

"What place?"

You tell him "the glasshouse."

"Are you kidding?" He explodes into pieces. You've never heard so many swear words. But you let them bounce off you as though they don't hurt a bit.

"She's not kidding," Josh tells him.

The three of you cross the road in a line, not greeting the Lollipop Man today. All of you have your hands in your pockets and are individually pulled in toward yourselves, fighting your own individual battles.

"I need to go home and show my dad this bruise so he can give me another to match it on the other cheek," Kevin says, and then he laughs as loud as he can. Neither of you laughs with him.

"Before you do, maybe you can say hello to Meixing's cat," says Josh.

The black-and-white cat is standing in the middle of the footpath on her hind legs. She is wearing a tuxedo that matches exactly the black-and-white patches on her body and is looking around casually.

"Why have you dressed your cat like this?" Kevin says in a puzzled voice. It at least has had the effect of taking the anger out of him.

"I don't know," you reply. "I think it's her choice."

The cat leads all three of you through the creaky

red gate with the heart-shaped eyes, down the trodden path, and to the door of the glasshouse, as if it were naturally supposed to be. She reaches up and turns the door handle with both paws. When you all still stand there, she shrugs her shoulders in annoyance and makes an arrow with her tail. You get the point.

"No, not this again," grumbles Kevin. "Don't expect me to be impressed or to have changed my mind."

Oh, it'll be different this time, you think to yourself, but you also understand that sometimes you have to let someone see for themselves.

You have been thinking about the incident with your cousins and Kevin and that you finally understand. None of you needed the glasshouse on that day. Biaomei and Biaojie might never need the glasshouse, and while you had them here, neither did you. Also as you remember it, Kevin was his usual sarcastic self, but armored and okay.

Right now nothing is okay. You all carry the weight of the world on your shoulders. You feel the blows, visible and on the inside, that have been dealt by the same hand. But you know that if you call on the glasshouse in your hour of need, the glasshouse—suspended somewhere between reality and imagination—will never let you down.

You lead your friends inside. The first thing that strikes you is how warm it is in here compared to the sharpness of winter outside.

You turn your head to look at Kevin, and you know, before you see his face, that it will be a mixture of confusion about why the glasshouse is so big on the inside and what is it with all the orange trees (there are now more than last time; Uncle must have been busy). But Kevin's face will also say that he always has low or no expectations about anything in this world and he never believed that the shelter you promised would actually be offered to him.

You are eager to see your flowers and your blue ornamental wisteria and Josh is eager to see his olive tree, so you run on ahead and let Kevin follow. The sun is slowly inching her way to the west, and the moon, having become new, is a transparent ghostly circle in the sky.

Since you were last here, your forget-me-nots have spread everywhere, even inside abandoned flowerpots under Uncle's planting station, the ones with a bit of leftover soil at the bottom. Your wisteria is so heavy with bloom, it is touching the ground and has formed the perfect hideaway for reading and drawing inside. Everything is so blue.

Josh looks up at his olive tree, which, in the funny time that exists here, has grown almost as old as the ones he remembers from a different home. You show Kevin the seed box, thinking that a tough boy like him surely wouldn't be interested in anything like gardening, which he probably thinks is for little kids or old people. But he surprises you by taking a long time looking over the seeds. Surely he will select the biggest one, the cocoa seed, which is the size of his head. Instead, he chooses a seed so small that at first you think his hand is empty.

He goes about planting and nurturing that seed in a way that makes you think he cares. You feel both happy and yet strangely sad at the same time. You think how vulnerable he looks. You don't think he ever lets anyone see this side of him.

The green shoot comes out of the ground and, from it, a bright red flower. In a single breath the flowers spread like wildfire all the way to the glass horizon. It is a slash of scarlet that clashes and sits uneasily next to your field of blue.

"What are they?" you ask Josh.

"Poppies," he replies.

"I feel sleepy."

"Me too."

"Kevin," you say, and you look around for him, but all you can see is red.

It is through a half-asleep haze that you watch the poppies tell the story. You see Kevin as a young boy with his parents, huddled together eating as much food as they can in one sitting. You understand when you see the long wooden boat that no one will get to eat again until they reach the other side of that great ocean.

You feel you can't stand anymore, so you get down on your knees in the soft dirt. Josh is already asleep, curled up on the dirt like a seed himself, thinking about sending roots into the soil below. You curl up next to him. You force yourself to keep your eyes open, and you see Mrs. Huynh give Kevin a large spoonful of cough medicine and tell him to close his eyes.

You want to close your eyes too and you feel yourself nodding off, but you jerk yourself from sleep to see Kevin wake up inside that long narrow boat and start to cry. Mrs. Huynh gives him another large spoon of cough medicine. The crying dies away and he is quiet.

"Kevin?" you say again. "Kevin, wake up!"

This time Kevin does not wake up and cry. He looks very pale and cold, rocking gently along with the boat. You get a very bad feeling, and you are back on your feet and running and screaming his name.

"Kevin! You gave me such a big scare!" He is at the edge of the poppies, sitting on his heels. When he looks up at you, you don't see that angry boy. You see through his armor, like a hole unraveled in a sweater, and you see a scared boy instead.

"I understand," you tell him, and you hold out your hand.

He doesn't let you help him up. Instead, he jumps up, and like that, you see that chink in his armor close up.

"You understand nothing about me!" Kevin turns and runs away from you and the glasshouse. The magic shatters.

Josh comes over and you both stare at the field of poppies together.

"When will he stop being so angry?" Josh asks, turning to you for an answer.

You don't have one, but you say, "The important thing is not to give up on him."

"Even if he's angry forever . . . ," says Josh, thinking as he says the words. Then he nods.

You wonder how, in the process of you all leaving

your homes and coming here, Josh has turned out so wise and Kevin has turned out so broken. You look up at the sky with the sun shining next to the almost invisible moon, and all you know is that humans are so complicated, and this is heartbreaking and heart-mending all at once.

CHAPTER TWENTY

Letter

The black-and-white gatekeeper insists on walking Josh home. You don't know what to do with Kevin. You look through the hole in the wooden fence, but his backyard is empty. There is a light on inside his house, making it glow warm and cozy, so you feel relieved. The feeling is quickly extinguished when you realize it was Mr. and Mrs. Huynh who decided to bring Kevin here on that dangerous journey that almost killed him.

You don't know why you feel you have to tiptoe when you go inside. You should have the right to stomp up and down the stairs banging on a pot if you want to, because it's your home too. But Ma Ma likes you quiet so you don't give her a headache.

She also doesn't like being touched, rarely gives and receives hugs, and doesn't want to be kissed like you see other kids kiss their parents at school drop-off. What type of rules are these? She says it is tradition. Which of your cold, uncaring ancestors is responsible? You want to scream!

Reluctantly, you check on her because she is still your mom.

Ma Ma is in her bedroom. Instead of lying on the bed, staring at the ceiling, she is now sitting on the edge, looking down at an envelope in her hand. You wouldn't be surprised if that is as far as she has moved all day. Her ankles look so swollen—the "heatiness" that First Aunty talked about must have returned, as Ma Ma's face is red. You suddenly feel sorry for her.

"Ma Ma, would you like the comfort drink you make for me when I get sick?"

"I'd like that very much," Ma Ma replies, looking down at the envelope. You don't think Ma Ma is sick. You don't think she is well, either. Since she has arrived at Big Scary, she has only left to go to the chicken place and the funeral parlor. This makes you think about Ba Ba again, so you hurry to the kitchen to make the drink. You have to keep yourself busy; cling to the hope that lies inside a pink cocoon in the corner of your bedroom window. A bell chimes once. You feel the eye in the Room on the Roof flutter open, then close.

The special drink is cocoa powder mixed with a splash of boiling water and topped with microwaved milk. You are reminded of what Ma Ma used to tell you: if a half crescent appears on the top of the foam, then it is a smile that means you will have a good day.

There is no smile today, no break on the surface. You arrange some biscuit-type crackers on the side, for dipping. It is not medicine, but it has never failed to fix you, whether you were in bed shivering from a cold or hot with fever, your face and forehead covered in your mother's cooling rice paste.

Ma Ma receives the hot chocolate gratefully, and you look at her making crumbs all over her big belly and feel the urge to brush them off her as though she's your child. You are not ready to switch roles if that is the way things have to be. You cannot rely on Mrs. Huynh for everything—and right now you don't know if you want to. You cannot be expected to buy the groceries and look after your mother and have to go to school at the same time. You just want to be a kid.

Tired of thinking, you sit down next to her and pick up the letter off the bed. It is old and yellowed by time. You turn it in your hands, trying to find the opening to the letter inside, but to your surprise, there isn't one. The letter has never been opened. You look at the words on the front, Old Language that you cannot read, and you think of the New Language you struggle with. And you mourn. You mourn for something you never had, because you cannot yet celebrate what you have not yet gained.

"Is this your letter, Ma Ma?"

"No. It belongs to your grandmother."

"And she didn't open it before she left?"

Ah Ma left the world a long time ago. Now she is only the face of the sad bride on the worst day of her life hanging on the wall, a frozen frame in time.

"No. It's because Ah Ma couldn't read."

"Then why would someone write her a letter?"

Ma Ma's eyes take on a fierce look and her lips turn up at the corners even though it isn't a smile.

"Your Ah Ma was smart, you know. She was very good at figuring out how things worked. She could look at how someone cooked a dish or sewed a piece of clothing and she would come home and do the same thing completely by memory. She even fixed an old radio by herself once. She just never had a chance to get an education."

Ma Ma looks to the side, out the window.

"But she was silly in the sense that she fell in love with a boy who, when he no longer loved her back, didn't have the guts to tell her. So he wrote it in a letter and then ran away."

"Oh." You put the letter back down on the bed.

Suddenly, Ma Ma is pulling you toward her.

"You know your stupid mother never got a

chance to have an education either. You learn all you can, Meixing. You go to school and you become like Ailing, okay? So if a silly boy ever writes you a letter, you can read it and you can write back the most brilliant reply calling him a fool. And he will know he is dealing with a strong woman."

Ma Ma is done and she lets go of you to wipe the snot away from her nose.

You are feeling stunned. You feel sad that Ma Ma called herself stupid because you know she's trying the best she can to read and write both the Old and New Language using her pocket translation dictionary. But you are too stunned to say anything. Ma Ma held you. And not only that, never in a million years would you think she had anything nice to say about Ailing.

"Ma Ma, I thought you hated Ailing? You don't even call her your sister."

Ma Ma gives you a genuinely surprised look from over her snotty hand.

"Have I ever said I hate Ailing? One day I know she will wonder why she is connected to a whole bunch of uneducated, loud, and crass women and she will disappear from our lives. I'm trying not to get too attached to her."

You pass Ma Ma a tissue and she gives a good blow into it.

"Will you promise you won't forget your Ma Ma when you are a Somebody one day?"

"Never," you say softly, and your eyes fill up with tears. You don't cry, though. Ma Ma is emotional and pregnant and it wouldn't be good for her to see. "I'll never forget."

That evening, even though all your aunts are gone, Mrs. Huynh does not come back. You look in the fridge and find a tray of *kueh* that Ailing had made. It didn't set properly and Ma Ma had been critical and told her to put it into the trash, but you think it's good enough for eating. It tastes delicious even though it slumps sideways and looks sad. You go about making Ailing's midnight meal: scrambled eggs on toast. Ma Ma does not think much of the New Land food, but she is hungry so she eats it anyway.

You go to stare at Ah Ma's wedding photo out in the formal dining room nobody ever uses and nobody even goes into. She stares at you with those brimming eyes and that straight mouth. You smile at her. She makes a little smile back at you.

Promise me you'll be the best writer one day, she asks of you.

I promise, you reply.

CHAPTER TWENTY-ONE

Stars

You wake up early to make Ma Ma another hot chocolate before school. In the corner of your window something inside the pink cocoon shifts, but then it goes quiet again. You press the coin inside your fist and call out to Ba Ba, asking him to follow the sound of the bell.

Big Scary's scales are so cold under your bare feet, but she tries to warm the ones you stand on long enough, chasing you around the kitchen with glowing pink squares. You stare at the urn that needs to be filled with five gallons of water, enough to make a hot drink for all your aunts, and it seems silly to still be using it. So you unplug it and put it away and take the kettle back out.

Breakfast is scrambled eggs on toast again, as it's the only thing you know how to cook. After you take out four eggs, there are only two eggs left inside the carton. This makes you panic, so you shut the lid quickly and put it away. You are not sure if you are brave enough to go to the grocery store by yourself.

There is also the problem of your uniform. You are down to your last clean shirt, jacket, and pair of pants. You look at the pile of dirty clothing in the laundry and, copying what you've seen done before, you turn all the clothes inside out, checking to make sure there are no tissues in the pockets. Then you throw them into the washer with a large scoop of powder. You turn it on and hope for the best.

Ma Ma eats her eggs gratefully. She seems sluggish and unable to get out of bed, so you put your palm on her forehead to see if she has a fever. She shakes your hand off irritably and says she is "not sick."

Maybe she needs to get checked out by someone who knows what they are doing. Maybe both she and the baby need to be checked out. But you don't know how you can make this happen.

On the way out you see Mrs. Huynh standing at her mailbox again. You come so close to asking her to go talk to Ma Ma. But you don't want to approach her only when you need her for something. You draw your shoulders up and walk away.

Ms. Jardine notices Kevin's bruise straight away.

He tells her he beat up an older kid and grins. She says she will talk to him about it later. Then she notices that there is something wrong with you, even though you don't have a bruise yourself, not one on the outside, anyway. It's almost as if she can tell by magic, just by looking at the way you sit and the way you hold your own body. Standing beside her bookshelves, she asks you to come over while the boys are busy working and to sit in a beanbag chair with her.

"This is my favorite book," she says, and hands it to you.

You open it and hold it in your lap. The sea of words inside makes your mind spin. But while it all attempts to overwhelm you, a few words you know jump out and, like little buoys upon that ocean, they keep you afloat. They remind you that you can kick and you can swim. Sentence to sentence.

"Something is worrying you," Ms. Jardine says. "Is it school? Or is it something else?"

You feel too nervous to look her in the face so you concentrate on the brooch she is wearing instead, a pair of lungs all studded with blue and red stones.

"Ma Ma," you say, and your throat feels so dry.

"Is Ma Ma not like she used to be?" asks Ms. Jardine.

You nod.

"And Ba Ba," you say.

"Is Ba Ba also not like he used to be?"

This is so hard. Tears form in your eyes.

"Ba Ba is gone in a car accident." The tears drop down onto your face.

"Oh no, I am so sorry," says Ms. Jardine, even though it is not her fault. "Let me ask a very important question, Meixing—do you feel like you are not how you used to be?"

"I feel different," you reply. "Some of it is a bad different."

"Have you told anyone else about this?"

"No," you reply, but now that you have told your teacher, it feels as though she is helping to lift the weight with you.

"I have a friend who can help. She is called a social worker, and she can come to your house after school and have a chat with you and Ma Ma. Does that sound okay?"

You nod.

"My friend won't be scary. She will probably bring some paper and supplies and ask you to draw pictures for her, like you do for me," Ms. Jardine says, and she squeezes your hand. You think you will be able to draw some pictures for this friend.

"Everything's going to be okay," says Ms. Jardine. You desperately hope so.

You try to talk to Kevin on the way back to normal class, but he races ahead of both you and Josh, and you can't catch him. Every time you go a little faster, he goes faster still. He swerves a completely different direction to the way you always take to get back. You and Josh look at each other in surprise until, still following Kevin, you realize he is avoiding the covered area of the schoolyard. You remember all too well what happened there last time.

Josh gives you an understanding glance as the two of you part to go to your own classrooms. You have never seen Kevin make a beeline for the door of class so fast.

"Kevin, I wish you would talk to me!" you shout at him.

He stops and turns. In shock, you think, as you've never raised your voice before. You've surprised yourself.

"Why? So you can try and understand me?" he spits out.

"Because we are friends. Remember what you said?" you reply.

"Don't be a loser." Kevin pulls open the door and

storms inside. You catch the door before it slams on your face. You watch as he marches not to his desk, but right up to where your former friend is sitting, smiling away with her other friends. You watch as he grabs her by the arm and drags it up to where he is. You watch in horror as he tries to twist your Ah Ma's ring off her finger.

"Kevin!" Miss Cicely screams. "What do you think you are doing! Let her go!"

"She is a thief! This is not her ring!" Kevin shouts as he finally tugs it free and holds it up in the air. Your former friend is squealing. Then she whacks Kevin right in the head.

"This is it! Kevin, principal's office!"

"But, Miss, she just hit me!"

"Shut up, you idiot boy!"

Kevin stops flailing around and sags on the spot. His face goes red, your face goes red, Miss Cicely's face is red too. Everyone else in the class stares in shock.

"This time you will be expelled."

Expelled. Sounds like something to do with casting magic spells.

This, though, is much too real.

"You want a 'thank you'? Here!" Kevin throws the ring at you. It bounces off your chest and rolls under your desk. Swiftly, you dive after it and hide it inside your fist. You turn to see Kevin marching out the door, this time successfully slamming the door behind him. You all jump.

"Give that to me," says Miss Cicely.

You want to tell her it belongs to you. It has always belonged to you, and before that it belonged to Ma Ma and Ah Ma before her. It is a precious family heirloom.

"Meixing, do you understand me?"

There is laughter behind you. You don't need to see who it comes from to know who it is.

You open your fist and hand Miss Cicely the ring. She glances at it and then puts it in the top drawer of her desk. You feel yourself losing again. Kevin is right, you are a loser. You want to quietly sit down and make yourself as small as possible so you don't lose any more.

"Please go to the principal's office."

Maybe you are an idiot as well because you don't understand her. You go to sit down.

"I said the principal's office, Meixing—now!"

You have never seen Miss Cicely so angry. You hurry quickly to the door and make sure it shuts politely behind you even though your hands are shaking uncontrollably. You think of Ma Ma telling you to stick it to the world and to be a strong woman—well, she says you have to be well mannered and meek too, so maybe you're always going to be weak.

The punishment wall is empty except for the cheerful graffiti. You walk up awkwardly past it and see that the principal's door is closed, so maybe Kevin is in there already. But peeking into the reception area, you see the back of the principal's head as he talks to the lady at the front desk. You quickly pull away, and you are walking across the grassed quadrangle and toward the school gate.

It is closed, but you push it open and you walk out.

"Kevin!"

Hands in his pockets, he has walked as far as the utility pole. He doesn't turn to the sound of your voice. It is so cold out here, you almost wish you were back in class.

"Kevin, please come back!"

He keeps walking.

"Don't be a loser!" you yell to get his attention.

He stops then and you catch up with him.

"You are not a loser, not even close. Please. Come back with me."

Kevin shakes his head at you. "If I go to the principal and get expelled, my parents will never forgive me. They always go on and on about the sacrifice they made to get me here and don't I know it!"

He holds his empty palms out. "Why am I like this?" he says, a little more quietly. "Sometimes I don't even understand myself."

You stare up at him. At his eye, almost knitted shut by the bruise.

"Let me help you. We can figure it out together."

"I can't go back," says Kevin.

"If we can't go back, we go forward," you finally say. "So let's go."

You grab his hand, and by the sheer will of your intentions you are both propelled forward. The Lollipop Man is not on the curb this time of day, but you both go flying across the road feeling as though a greater force is ferrying you safely to where you need to go. The shame of Ma Ma and Mrs. Huynh catching you both crosses your mind, but you push it away. *I need to be here; I need to do this. I am sorry, but I'm also not sorry.*

The black-and-white gatekeeper is at the open door of the glasshouse, hauling out a large harvest of a very pungent-smelling herb. *Catnip,* she says without moving her mouth.

Your field of blue flowers and Kevin's field of red flowers sit side by side under the slightly pinking sky, the sun now in the west. The moon is full again. You sit next to Kevin at the edge with your legs crossed, and your forget-me-nots tell him a story of memories.

About a grandmother who could not read and the letter addressed to her. About a mother who could also not read and the dream that her daughter one day would. And not only read! Her daughter was going to read in the New Land, where she had the chance of the best life. The forget-me-nots tell the story of a daughter who could read a little but bore the weight of all the women who came before her on her shoulders, like a very difficult acrobatic act.

Kevin looks over and you think he understands why you are blue.

He picks one of the sleepy poppies from the field and presses it into your palm. You close your hand around it and hold it to your heart, and your eyelids become heavy. You fight to keep them open, but they close. When you open them again, you open them in the ghost world.

The younger Kevin in the long wooden boat has become cold and slack, and Mrs. Huynh cannot wake him. You feel her rising panic, as there have been those on board who have fallen into slumbers that last forever. They are unceremoniously wrapped in white sheets and put into the ocean.

Wake up, you tell the younger Kevin. The cough medicine swirls in his stomach that has been empty for five days.

You see the poppies fluttering behind the red of your eyelids. You see Mrs. Huynh take a crumpled photo from her pocket. It is the face of a toddler, but it is not the face of Kevin. She wipes away a tear and tucks the photo back in her shirt. This child is not on the boat with them, and you understand that this child will always stay the same age as in the photo. You understand now that this is why the Huynhs needed to get away to a land where there is enough to eat.

But it will be to no avail if Kevin cannot wake up. You shake him, and suddenly he is sick and the cough medicine dribbles out of his mouth and swirls on the bottom of the long wooden boat. But he is finally awake. And the boat has hit the shore.

You have reached the end of your journey, but it is only the beginning. Of cyclone fencing and barbed wire spirals and a cage where you will all stay until it becomes so long that you call it home. Even though it is a jail and not a home at all. Inside you rage and shout and your blood boils over.

You look over at Kevin and you understand why he is red.

"You don't have to fight me," you say, and you take both his hands in yours.

As soon as you connect, a new color sweeps through both of your fields at the same time and they are no longer blue and red. All the flowers have become asters; all the flowers are purple.

Above you the moon begins to move across the sky and over the face of the sun. As a complete eclipse occurs, the whole world becomes black.

"Are you scared of the darkness?" Kevin asks you.

"No," you say.

With your answer, the black sky is at once filled with a million galaxies.

It is the most beautiful thing you have ever seen.

"No," you repeat. "Because you can only see the stars when it is dark."

And like that, you go from being a girl and a boy fighting yourselves and each other to a pair of friends fighting the world. You both sigh and let go of each other and fall to the earth on your backs. You stare at the stars and you tell Kevin the story of the weaver girl and the lonely cowherd, banished to opposite ends of the galaxy, but how the stars became the Milky Way between them.

Kevin says he is glad to have met you. It is good to have a friend.

CHAPTER TWENTY-TWO

Frogs

Your mother is wild with worry when you go back inside Big Scary. She tells you that the school called and she feared the worst. Because she couldn't understand the man on the other end, she had to wait till they called back with an interpreter. This took a long time, and during that time she was still fearing the worst. Then the interpreter called and her worst fears were finally realized, but the lead-up to it was somewhat worse.

You listen with a mixture of shame and confusion. You are genuinely upset with yourself for not thinking that your absence from school would be noticed; that they would contact your pregnant mother who thought you had been taken by a bad person or come to harm. But then you wonder why she sat inside all this time with this information. Why she didn't go outside and start looking for you. Why, now that you are back, she is standing such a great distance away from you.

Big Scary's walls seem to be moving in. But Ma Ma feels miles away.

"You have to go straight to the principal's office first thing tomorrow. You can't get into trouble; you just can't, Meixing," she pleads. "Think of your poor mother."

You know that. Tears pinch at your eyes and bitterness squeezes the corners of your mouth.

There is a sudden knock on the door. Both of you freeze.

Ma Ma puts a finger to her lips. She moves to the window and you follow behind. She peers through the drawn curtain. You kneel down and peek timidly through the same gap of the heavy brocade fabric. There is a lady standing there, dressed in a neat suit and holding a briefcase.

You are certain that this is the person Ms. Jardine said is her friend. You should let her in. She's here to help. She will tell you why the two of you aren't the same as you used to be. Why Ma Ma doesn't want to leave the house at all.

Ma Ma, though, puts her finger back on her lips and a firm hand on your shoulder.

You watch as the lady knocks on the door again.

You stare straight at her, hoping that she might turn and see both your faces in the gap of the curtain. She looks behind her. *Look at me,* you beg. Finally, she scribbles something on a little card and tucks it into the screen door, turns, and makes the journey down those thirty steps. You really want to call out to her, but your voice catches in your throat.

Ma Ma seems relieved. She goes back to her bedroom and lies down on the bed.

Numb, you go into the kitchen and open the fridge. The brown-and-orange eyes stare questioningly up from the tiles in the kitchen and close when you tread on them with your bare feet. You study the two remaining eggs in the carton. You take one out and scramble it, put it on a plate with toast and load it onto the serving tray with another hot chocolate and biscuits. Ma Ma eats her dinner in bed, a bolster pillow tucked under her knees. She doesn't ask you why you are not eating.

You have the most terrible feeling of dread in your body. But you hold yourself together because you still have to take the wet clothes out of the washer, put them into the spinner, and then hang them outside. You don't know how long you can hold the two of you together by yourself.

You sit on your bed that night and look out the

window while the pink cocoon remains silent in the corner. The rag doll you had tried to discard is rediscovered and you stroke her face gently. Big Scary fills the room with a pink light and you feel safe and sound, even though you will have to face the principal tomorrow. You look down at what you're holding in your hand—the card that Ms. Jardine's friend left in the door.

There is no improvement in Ma Ma's condition the following day. She is lucid and awake and seems happy enough to see your face at her bedroom door, but this is not the Ma Ma who once belonged to you. The one who lived on the island home with you another lifetime ago. Who loved to be at the ocean and who drove Ba Ba's beat-up dune buggy without a license like a woman possessed. You feed her the last egg for breakfast.

You think of Ba Ba with a type of clarity you weren't capable of even a week ago. You remember how he came home one day with a ridiculous rainbow-striped waistcoat that his boss on the island had given him. Ma Ma groaned and you laughed, but Ba Ba wore it all the time until he just stopped one day. That was when you realized how much you would miss the ugly thing and how you shouldn't have made bad jokes about it. You miss him so much. But you smile.

You wash the dishes. You sweep the floor. You have run out of things to make for lunch.

When you throw open the front door, you are shocked to see what awaits you at the bottom of the staircase. It is Kevin.

"What are you doing?"

"Seeing if you want to walk to school together— what does it look like?" he says, his usual gruff self. He stomps on the bottom step of Big Scary with displaced energy.

"Ow!" A gumnut has dropped out of the sky and onto his head—the problem being that there are no gum trees where he is standing. Big Scary is laughing.

"I would like to do that," you answer.

Kevin scratches the back of his head nervously. You think he is wearing gel in his hair. Both of you walk very slowly toward school. When you turn your heads to greet the Lollipop Man, now a friend almost, you sneak a look at Kevin's bruise. It looks better.

"Ready to fight for our rights?" he asks as you arrive at the punishment wall.

You nod. You and him. Against the world.

The principal's door opens and a voice calls your names.

In your imagination the principal has taken on the proportions of a monster, with canes on the ends of each of his fingers that he is not allowed to use. What type of lair would he be inhabiting in there? Maybe he lives in an all-concrete cell; sitting on a nest made of confiscated children's hair, with bits of eraser and broken pencils he has collected and woven in like a macabre keepsake.

Kevin holds the door open for you, and you take a deep breath and enter.

Mr. Jones surprises you, firstly by being human. The slight, grey-haired man with a smile on his face disarms you. Like Ms. Jardine, he wears a pin on the left-hand side of his collar, a rainbow. His office is also grey, but neat, with a framed photo of a dog in one corner.

"Hello, Kevin. Nice to see you again. As for you, Meixing, nice to finally meet you."

He holds out his hand over the desk and you take it. He gives you a firm shake.

"Now, I have been seeing a lot of you lately, young man. In fact, due to the severity of your behavior—assaulting another student—I have no choice but to follow school policy and suspend you."

Kevin hangs his head. "I think you should."

"A few days at home to think about your actions will do you good."

"Yes, sir."

"But, I have some positive news."

Kevin looks back up, but he does not look hopeful.

"I have been speaking with Ms. Jardine, and she reports that you, and Meixing too, have been progressing very positively. So I am arranging for there to be more class contact hours between all of you. Starting today, this morning."

Your eyes widen and you try to catch Kevin's attention, but he is looking back at his feet again. So you quietly rejoice on the inside instead.

"Now, Meixing. The reason why I brought you in with Kevin is that this story appears to be interconnected. Can you explain it to me? In your words, please."

If someone had asked you that two weeks or even one week ago, you would have probably burst into tears like you had done once before. But you are stronger now, and slowly and steadily, you compose your words so that they are just right.

"The girl in the class stole my ring. Kevin took it back off her to return to me. He tried to do the honorable thing. I understand he hurt her, but if not for me, he wouldn't be here."

You press your lips together and clasp your fingers in your lap.

"I believe you, Meixing." Mr. Jones opens his top drawer and takes something out. He holds his closed hand out across his desk and nods to you. You reach your palm over. In it he drops Ah Ma's gold ring.

Your mouth opens, and you hold the ring so tight in your fist that nobody will be able to pry it from you ever again. You feel a tiny piece of strength, like a piece of armor, attach itself to your soul. It's as if you are staring straight into your future and can imagine that, one day, you'll grow into a strong woman with a whole suit of armor. Not like Kevin's to keep people out, but like a shield to go with the glittering magic sword you will hold high up in the air.

"Which brings me to say, I'm going to have to call young Paige to my office to explain why she had your ring. We don't tolerate theft at this school."

If you had the ability at that point to say "thank you," you would, but you are so overwhelmed that you can only mouth the words. You think of how you've met some not-so-very-nice people since coming to the New Land, but you've also met wonderful, just, and kind people, because there will always be good people everywhere.

"I think Paige's parents might be interested to hear all about this story. And I think she might learn some good old-fashioned values like honesty by picking up rubbish during lunchtimes, what do you think? I'm not cruel, I do hand out stickers afterward."

You try to hide a smile.

"You can go back to class now, Meixing."

"I'm sorry," you whisper into Kevin's ear.

"It's okay. When I get angry and I see red, I try to think of that field of purple," he says softly back.

"As for you, Kevin," says the principal, "you can stay in my office until your parents come and fetch you. But I promise I will explain everything very fairly to them."

Kevin lets out a loud sigh. You are still worried, but he seems calm and is not looking as though he is about to punch any walls.

"Do you like gummy frogs?" Mr. Jones asks Kevin, opening his top drawer again.

"Only the red ones."

"Well, you're in luck. They are the ones I like too," you hear Mr. Jones reply as you quietly leave the office and click shut the door.

Ms. Jardine looks worried and not her smiling self today. Her face is as gloomy as the black pupil of the eyeball brooch on her woolly cardigan.

"I asked my friend to go over to your house yesterday after you went missing," she says to you. "But nobody was home. Is everything okay?"

You don't want to worry Ms. Jardine because

you want to see her smile and her sunshine come back. But you don't know what name to put on the invisible monster that seems to be wrapping itself around Ma Ma and making her shoulders, body, and entire being sag; sitting so heavy on top of her in bed and keeping her there.

"I will try to get my friend to visit again another time, okay?"

You nod.

"She only wants to talk to you and your mother. She won't do anything scary, I promise."

You nod again.

"Can I trust that you will open the door for her, Meixing?"

You don't know.

You want Ms. Jardine to help you. You want to tell her everything. You want to tell her your story, right from the start. But you keep it all inside and don't say a thing because it has nothing to do with the reason you're in this class; nothing to do with spelling, grammar, or language.

Ms. Jardine tries to smile for you. She touches the bottom of your chin gently and then flicks back into teacher mode, going over the answers that you got right and wrong on your last exercise. She explains everything so carefully and kindly, you wish you could promise her that you'll let her friend in.

Josh taps you on the shoulder and asks what is wrong. You feel as though your heart is beating a million miles per minute and you can't seem to slow it down. It's as though you are nervous or scared about something even though you are safe inside Ms. Jardine's rickety little classroom.

You are powerless to control the feeling, and it threatens to turn you into a sad blue girl again. This is when you close your eyes and concentrate all your energy on bringing that field of asters into your mind. Like Kevin, you fight it with that wave of purple. But some things are much bigger than you. You don't know what is wrong with Ma Ma. You don't know what is wrong with you, either.

Josh draws you a picture of a girl sitting inside a glass bowl, with a goldfish looking into it from the outside. You turn the girl's legs into the bottom half of a mermaid. You draw a party hat and a party horn on the goldfish. You get a laugh out of Josh. He adds a little crown on the girl.

"I miss Kevin," says Josh.

"I do too," you reply.

You sit together at lunchtime, still missing Kevin, but smiling behind the food Josh is sharing with you. You don't seem to care as much anymore that you are still sitting on the edge of the assembly area. It is not such a bad view.

Your former friend is trailing behind the principal, trying to pretend she is not associated with him. Mr. Jones points to a piece of rubbish on the ground.

"I'm not touching that trash!" She scowls and turns her nose up.

"Keep the country beautiful," says Mr. Jones, and he points to it again.

"I'm a model," she says. When he is unmoved, she says more quietly, "It might make me sick . . . it might give me diarrhea!"

But everyone hears it. She is forced to pick the rubbish up anyway. Her friends suddenly don't know her. The boys laugh at her. Mr. Jones remains true to his word and offers her a sticker when the bell rings, even though she rejects it.

Ah Ma's ring is firmly on your finger. You look at Josh, and he smiles back at you with a dimple in his cheek. You wonder what "diarrhea" means.

Your former friend is quiet for the rest of the day, and it comes as a sweet relief.

CHAPTER TWENTY-THREE

Groceries

There's something wrong with Big Scary. She looks dark in the face, as though she's been punched. The Room on the Roof sits like a bruised eye. You slip your backpack off and hold it tight in front of you. It seems to weigh a ton, like a boulder, like the sinking feeling in your stomach.

All the curtains are closed.

Big Scary looks down at you with her one purple eye.

This has fast become the worst part of any day. Coming home.

You stare back up at her, and she blinks once but keeps looking at you.

Slowly, you trudge up the thirty steps with your eyes on her. She keeps her eye on you. You feel her eye still on you as you open the front door.

You almost knock Ma Ma right over.

"Oh! I am so sorry! Ma Ma, what are you doing?"

She has a paintbrush in her hand and a small half-used tin of paint, the same creamy color as on the walls upstairs. She is in the process of painting over the amber window in the front door. As she applies another blob of paint onto the glass, you see it visibly recoil. You feel Big Scary pull herself in farther. Ma Ma finishes painting over the entire window. You hear the house make a loud creaking noise filled with splinters and cracking wood. You think Big Scary might be crying.

"I don't want people looking in—it's none of their business," says Ma Ma.

She goes to all the windows and pulls the curtains tighter together to hide the gaps in the middle, turning on the lights as she makes the house darker.

Suddenly, the phone rings. Ma Ma drops the tin of paint and it hits the floor. Specks fly onto the wood-paneled walls and onto Big Scary's fur in the adjacent living room. Paint from the tipped can slowly trickles out; the tiles underneath shift faster. Ma Ma freezes, and you freeze too. The phone keeps on ringing. Ma Ma seems unable to move, so you pick up the paint tin and stand it back up. The phone stops ringing; there is a click, and the wheels of the tape inside the answering machine start to spin.

"Go and lie down, Ma Ma," you tell her.

As silent as a ghost, she disappears from the room. You go to the linen cupboard to fetch old towels and to the laundry room to get a mop and bucket, and you clean up the mess as best you can. As you wipe down the walls, Big Scary pulses pink for you and you press your palm against her. You want to wipe the paint off the window in the front door, but you don't dare.

The egg carton in the fridge is now empty. You close it and then open it up in hope, but magic is unpredictable and moves in mysterious ways and it can't help you with that. There is no milk left and no more bread.

Kneeling down beside the answering machine, you press the button with the single arrow to see what happens.

You have one new message, the machine announces in its mechanical tone.

Then a familiar voice fills the air.

"Hello? This is Ailing. Ah . . . I'm just ringing to check that everything has been okay since we left. I hope the two of you are coping in that great big house . . . I think about both of you all the time."

Ailing clears her throat as if she felt the last sentence was a rather silly thing to say.

"Anyway, if it's not too much to ask, I am thinking

about coming back soon. I mean, I don't mind if I have to stay at a hotel . . . if I might be considered too much of an intruder . . ."

Her voice trails off sadly.

"I'll try ringing another time. Bye."

The line goes dead.

Come back, Ailing! you shout in your head. The machine wants to know if you'd like to listen to the message again, so you listen to it another two times, as if it is a lifeline to the outside world. You wish Ailing would call again. That if you hope hard enough it might just happen and you will pick up the receiver in joy. But the phone stays silent.

"We have to go out and buy some food," you say to Ma Ma.

She is lying in bed with the covers over her, all bunched up into one corner. She turns over heavily, like a whale in water, and looks up at you, but she doesn't move.

"Please, Ma Ma," you say with a heavy heart.

There is a knock on the front door. Ma Ma freezes, and again you freeze with her. Maybe it is Ms. Jardine's friend. You have to let her in. You have to trust that Ms. Jardine's friend will help both of you.

"Please don't open the door," whispers Ma Ma, her eyes begging you.

"But why, Ma Ma?"

"I can't face the world," says Ma Ma, and her lips turn down.

"Okay. I promise."

As quietly as you can, you tiptoe to the front and peep out between the curtains.

It is Mrs. Huynh.

You are so relieved to see her, you want to let her in immediately so she can help solve this terrible situation you are both in. But then you think of Ma Ma's words and you grow silent. You swallow the lump in your throat as you watch a visibly confused Mrs. Huynh leave. You press your palm hard against the windowpane as you watch her descend the thirty steps.

There is a movement behind you and Ma Ma is also at the window. She sees Mrs. Huynh reach the bottom of the steps and she doesn't say a thing.

"Meixing?"

You look at her; her hair disheveled and her eyes rubbed red.

She drops down onto her knees next to you. "I'm so sorry, Meixing. I'm finding it very hard to cope."

You brush Ma Ma's hair off her sticky face.

"We have to go to the shops," you say to her. "Remember what I said, we need to get more food."

215

You look into her eyes, all funny and glassy. You are sure she can see you, but unsure she's not seeing straight through you.

"There are plenty of cans and jars in the pantry—we can live on those," Ma Ma says finally.

"I need bread and chicken slices and yogurt for school. You need me to go to school, right? Isn't that why we came here?"

Your mother nods, but she still looks confused at the same time.

"We can go straight to the shops and back again. We don't have to talk to anyone. We can keep our heads down."

Your mother nods again and blinks in quick succession.

"Where is your bag, Ma Ma?"

You help her find her wallet, place it into her handbag, and put the strap over her head.

"Let's go."

You open the front door and help Ma Ma step over the threshold, careful not to tread on the god living there, and out onto the porch. Then, drawing breath at each step and letting it out, you help her down those thirty steps. Like Ba Ba last helped her down.

"Are you sure this will be safe?"

"Of course, Ma Ma."

"I keep thinking about the last time I went outside. Meixing, please tell me that nothing bad is going to happen this time."

"Nothing bad is going to happen."

Ma Ma smiles and looks a little better. All you are going to do is walk down the street. There is a corner store at the very end that Ailing would walk to every morning to buy a newspaper and fresh flowers for her room. You will buy a few things and then head straight back.

As you both start walking, the remaining fears dissolve. As you go past the Huynhs' place, you stare at it wistfully. You wish that you could go over and hang out, or that Kevin could come over to your place so you could both just act like children. Instead, he is somewhere behind that closed door, carrying the weight of his parents' expectations on his shoulders. As you are carrying the weight of Ma Ma's on yours. You hope that he isn't being punished too badly.

"That's it. A little bit farther," you say. You feel dizzy, as though the world has been picked up and shaken violently and things have become all confused and mixed up. You have now become Ma Ma and Ma Ma has become a baby. When the cocoon in your bedroom opens, your father will come out and become a moth.

You go past a man and woman walking their dog, but you keep your head down like you promised Ma Ma, and they don't try to say hello or talk to you. Their dog sniffs Ma Ma's leg and she cries out in surprise, but you hurry her along and the dog is pulled back on his leash.

Ma Ma is right, we don't need any help. We can fix this by ourselves. We can take care of each other, you think to yourself.

You keep walking. If you concentrate on walking and don't think of anything else, then sooner or later you will get there. And you do. Up ahead in the distance, on the other side of the street, you can see a bright pink wraparound sign with white cursive writing that reads *Ice Cream Snacks Hot Food Flowers*. You are proud you can read all the words!

Entering the front door, pushing past straps of plastic that hit you in the face, you find a tiny store crowded inside with shelves and shelves of food. Some of the cans, cartons, and packets look similar to the things in the general store back on the island, but there are things you have never seen before.

Ma Ma is entranced by the strange cakes and sweets in the glass display, especially a rectangle of pink-colored coconut with bits of cherry glaze, sandwiched between two pieces of dark chocolate. You stare at the endless types of candy, all wrapped in individual cellophane bags. You pick one up that has six red jelly frogs inside and show it to Ma Ma. She opens her wallet and counts the coins and says you deserve a treat.

Onto the front counter goes a loaf of bread, milk, eggs, chicken slices, and the bag of candy. The lady who rings up the bill says hi and tries to engage in conversation, but you both lower your heads and feel like you can't talk back. Your groceries go into a paper bag and you pick it up in your arms, whisper, "Thank you," and hope that the lady heard you.

Outside, walking back home, feeling a little more confident and relaxed, Ma Ma affectionately touches the top of your head.

"Thank you, Meixing. I'm sorry I didn't trust you."

You smile and say it's okay. She holds the bag of groceries while you open the packet of red frogs and curiously bite into one. It is sweet and chewy and the yummiest thing you have ever eaten. You offer one to Ma Ma, but she shakes her head. You quietly try to figure out how many you should save for Kevin.

You are almost home and almost safe.

Until you see the three teenage boys up ahead.

What scares you are the heavy black combat boots. They look like they are made for kicking and stomping things. What those things are, you don't know. They are huddled around a utility pole. The boy with the shaved head has his back to you. Your instincts tell you something is wrong. Your body is flooded with a cold numbness followed by bursts of your heart pumping, as if giving you the choice to stay or to run.

CHAPTER TWENTY-FOUR

Boots

If you hold your breath and try to breeze past them in *one swift motion, it might be okay,* you tell yourself. You know you should turn around and go back to the store, ask the lady there for help. But you are too proud to have to admit to Ma Ma that you were wrong, that the world is unsafe and scary. You don't want to believe it yourself. At that moment you know you are pinning a lot on a tiny hope. But you grab on to that hope against hope and you approach closer. You just want to go home.

The boy with the shaved head turns and sees the two of you and grins broadly.

All we can do is keep going, you think to yourself. Head down. Walk fast. Clear this one section of footpath and you will both be across and it will be over. Home is up ahead.

The three boys spread out and block the footpath.

You slow down. Instinctively, you put yourself in front of Ma Ma.

They cannot block the way like that. There are other people around. It is very cold, but it's not raining so people are out and about. Walking their dogs. Exercising. Going to work. Leaving work. Surely one of them will come along and tell them to move.

There might be other people around, but nobody comes to help you.

It is much too late when you realize they are holding the yellow flyers.

"I think you should go home," says the teenager with the shaved head.

You don't dare look at his face, but you recognize the same features as that boy from school, the one who had the same flyer, who said he had an older brother. This is a scary new experience, but it feels all too familiar.

You stare at a crack in the concrete. Try not to notice the heavy black boots. You look at your feet and they look so small.

You are not sure what is on Ma Ma's face because you don't dare look at her. You take the grocery bag back from her, as if it might form some sort of pathetic shield.

The teenager then says a word that you haven't

heard before. He spits it out with a pure hatred you have never experienced. His friends laugh. Grasping Ma Ma's wrist firmly, you sidestep to the right so that you can go around the footpath. Your mind screams for you to go back, but you tell yourself you need to go forward.

The heavy black boots sidestep onto the grass as well.

Then a heavy hand lands on your shoulder, dropped on you so hard that you are almost hammered into the ground. The bag of groceries goes tumbling down. The breath is knocked out of your lungs so you can't even scream. You don't think you could anyway. A soft pair of hands pulls you away, and you hear Ma Ma yell, "Run!"

Like that, the adrenaline kicks in and you are pounding the pavement, the sound of your breathing and your heart beating inside your ears. You run as fast as you can, even though your knees are jelly and your shoulder is stinging. It feels like one of those nightmares where you can't run fast enough.

Ma Ma.

You stop and turn around. Ma Ma is not behind you. She is still all the way back with the three teens in the black boots, like the light at the end of a very long, dark tunnel.

"Ma Ma," you shout, and you go to run back.

"Stay where you are, Meixing!" she shouts back.

The teens howl at her Old Language.

Ma Ma.

She says that your grandmother, although illiterate, was clever in other ways. She says she is illiterate too, but unfortunately also simpleminded. But Ma Ma is the smartest person you know.

She takes the handbag off her shoulder and hurls it as hard as she can at the boy with the shaved head. Then, cradling her big belly, she runs as fast as she can manage toward you, screaming for you to keep running on ahead.

You see the gang staring in your direction, but they do not follow. They pick up Ma Ma's handbag and you watch them shake it out violently onto the pavement. Ma Ma's reading glasses and her pocket translation dictionary come rolling out. You watch as they pick up her wallet.

Ma Ma's hand clasps tightly on to yours and you both hurry home.

She is shaking and doubled over when you reach the bottom of the steps. A horrible thin noise, full of pain and fear, is coming out of her mouth.

You can see Big Scary's eye open wide in surprise, darting around and blinking, but focusing on nothing.

"Just these thirty steps," you beg Ma Ma, and she stops moaning and goes very quiet.

You put your arms around her, supporting her weight as you heave her up onto the first step. She gives a strange cry as her feet hit the stone. She makes this sound each time she mounts another step. You silently start counting from one all the way to thirty. With each number, you swear you are not going to make it.

One. You are weak. *Two.* Your mother has lost her strength. *Three four five six ten and twenty.* By the grace of some force that has not forgotten you, you make it to the top step. *Thirty.*

Squeezing back into the front door that seems smaller than when you left, you both stagger inside.

For years and years after, you will have the same nightmare. You will fill your head with fantasies hoping to erase the memory. In one of these rewrites of the story, Ba Ba comes along and cracks the heads of the gang together, sending them packing as you cheer. In another, it is you who screams and runs right at your attackers, punching them in that place at your height where it hurts.

These wishful scenarios will haunt you for the rest of your life, even after you are grown and feel strong and confident in yourself. Long after the bruise on your shoulder has healed. Long after you have patched up the wounds of your childhood. Some things leave a mark.

You help a limping Ma Ma into her bedroom and into the middle of the bed. She doesn't know how to make herself comfortable. She tries to lie down. Turns over on both sides. Tucks a pillow between her legs. Lies back down. Sits back up again. Eventually, she slides down onto Big Scary's fur and drapes her arms over the top of the mattress, as though she is sinking and holding on to it for dear life, in case it floats away.

There is a disturbance, like the hum of a bow upon cello strings. Like the creaking of a huge ship coming apart or a large house contracting.

You feel it as strange rooms with strange purposes—like the one with a deep square spa and the one with only a grand piano in it—break off and disappear without a trace. Big Scary is taking herself apart and packing up as if she intends to leave this time.

You crouch down next to your mother. The two of you kneel as if you are praying, but to what in this hopeless New Land, you don't know. You feel your whole face collapsing, but no tears come. You wish they would, but you are completely empty.

"Ma Ma, I am so sorry!" you burst out saying.

"Meixing, did you not hear me when I said to run?"

You did. You ran away like a coward and left your pregnant mother behind. They could have hurt her. You failed your mother.

"Old Ma Ma doesn't matter, don't apologize," she says to you, her eyes shining. "I told you to run because you are the one who matters. That's why we came here, Meixing."

And suddenly, you don't feel so much like it is an impossible expectation you have to live up to, but rather, a simple act of love.

Ma Ma wraps her arms around you, and you both shiver in the tiny, cold room as it slowly shrinks.

"Was all your money inside that purse, Ma Ma?"

"Yes."

"What are we going to do?"

"It is only money. We have each other." The words come out of Ma Ma's mouth in puffs of smoke that hang in the air. It is getting colder.

"What does the word 'diarrhea' mean, Ma Ma?" you blurt, trying to take your mind off things.

"I don't know, but the translation dictionary will."

She crawls over to her bedside drawer and removes a large, well-thumbed leather book with the Old Language printed on the front in gold lettering.

"Let me see." Ma Ma flips through it as you both try to sound out the word together. "Surely another useful New Land word to add to what I know."

She runs her finger down the page and stops at the right word. She reads the translation.

A smile plays on her downturned lips and a light comes on inside her tired eyes. Then Ma Ma starts laughing and can't stop even when she starts to choke. You have to thump on her back. When she tells you what is so funny and laughs at the shocked look on your face, you start laughing too. You both laugh until tears stream down your cheeks, and unsure of whether you are happy or sad anymore, you cling to each other so tight.

When Ma Ma falls asleep shortly after, you pad down the neglected hallway as the dust bunnies made of lint and fluff try to escape from under your feet. You open the front door, shut it behind you, and go slowly down the staircase.

Quiet as possible, because you want to be invisible, you slowly retread the same path, hoping that you can find Ma Ma's handbag and what is left of the groceries. You wish you were Ailing, bustling down the pavement every morning, not giving the world a second thought. Maybe one day.

The utility pole has been decorated with a single yellow flyer and it stops you in your tracks. For a split second, from a distance, it looks like the talisman Ba Ba stuck inside Big Scary to keep the bad monsters out. You shake your head and the flyer goes back to looking like a warning to stay away.

The handbag and the groceries are gone. The only thing that remains is smashed eggs. You poke them with your shoe and turn to go home, your stomach sore from the worry about dinner rather than from any real hunger.

Dragging your feet, your shoulders sagging, you almost trip over what has been left on the bottom step of Big Scary.

The bag of groceries.

It is the same paper bag, judging by the smeared egg stains on one side, but it has been refilled with fresh food. A fresh carton of eggs. A fresh loaf of bread. Sitting on the top is Ma Ma's handbag.

It is magic.

No, it is only human kindness.

You hear a "psst" and turn around to see Mrs.

Huynh standing by her mailbox. Your hand goes up automatically to your body. Before you have a chance to say anything, not even "thank you," she has hurried back into her home. When you look down, you realize you have placed your palm over your chest. Your heart is aching. But in the best way.

CHAPTER TWENTY-FIVE

Petals

Before dark Ma Ma lets out a scream unlike any that you have heard before and she clutches her belly. Big Scary groans in unison and shrinks away. Ma Ma calls for you to bring her some towels.

"I think the baby is coming." She doubles down in pain again.

You hurry out to find the towels. In your panic you look around the laundry room, the kitchen; you can't look in the linen closet because it has disappeared. Big Scary is leaving right now. You are afraid that the bedroom door is going to close upon Ma Ma.

"I know that you are scared," you say to Big Scary as you touch her wall. "Please don't be. I'm scared too."

There is a crack, and the window in the front door shatters. You jump and take a step back. The painted shards fall off. You look around in desperation. You need help, *now*. Throwing open the front door, you run down the front steps.

At the Huynhs' place you bang on the door. No one answers you. You bang on it again twice as desperately. But there is no noise on the other side.

Mrs. Huynh. Mr. Huynh. Kevin. Where are you all? I need you.

You look over at Big Scary. You have to go back. You have run out of time.

Big Scary looks smaller than she's ever been, and as you get closer, she seems to be moving farther away toward the horizon. It's then you realize with horror that she will soon be the size of a dollhouse; any hesitation and she will be gone.

You run quickly up the staircase. Big Scary covers her face with her long cactus fingers in fear. The door has shrunk to half its size, so you get on your knees and crawl inside. It is terribly cold inside and also very dark.

"Hello?" you whisper, and the word echoes around the walls.

You rush toward the bedroom, but Ma Ma is not there.

A layer of frost is forming on all the furniture. The windowpanes are white and blind.

"Hello?"

You don't know if you are talking out loud or inside your head or what is real and what is just your imagination and if you are writing this story or it is writing you.

There is no answer at all.

You run into the kitchen and then directly to the dining room, but the dining room is in the act of disappearing. You make a dash for the door, but it's too late and you come face-to-face with a blank wall.

Is the staircase going to disappear too? You rush to the bottom of it and touch your hand to the banister. The icicles that have formed all the way to the top tremble and clink together. Then the entire thing shatters like glass. Backing away, you look around desperately. You know instinctively, on the inside, that you have to go up. But you have reached the end this time. You have come so far, but all opportunities are gone now.

Until you dig a little deeper. You remember your secret spiral staircase. The one that connects the adults to the children. It is still standing. You don't wait around for it to disappear—two, three, four steps at a time you sprint upward, breathing deeply, clouds falling out of your mouth.

There is not much left of the upstairs now, not much of the landing to stand on.

You watch as the last remaining spare rooms melt away and the handrail disappears from under your hand like mist.

Until nothing remains but your bedroom.

It feels like ice when you enter. Your palms are so white that the three lines determining your life, heart, and fate are etched clearer than ever. Your bed is still there and so is your rag doll. You pick her up and hold her close to your heart. Ma Ma made her for you when she had nothing else to give you. And for that, you will love her more than any fancy plastic horse.

The only sign of life is the cocoon in the corner of the window, gently trembling.

Then somewhere inside the ceiling you hear the muffled voice of your mother.

"Ma Ma!" you shout. You stand up on your bed to find the sound, but it is gone.

"Meixing, my amazing girl." Ma Ma's voice comes in loud, but just as suddenly fades away. You try to jump from your bed to touch the ceiling, but it is out of the reach of your fingertips.

A bell rings. The air becomes very clear and very pure. There is a scratching noise, maybe inside your head. Something is hatching. You turn to see the little pink cocoon twisting and moving. It is struggling, and your first instinct is to go over and help, but something inside tells you that whatever is coming needs to come out by itself.

Hours seem to pass as you stare transfixed—or is it days? You cannot tell because the room is lit by neither natural nor artificial light, but internally from within. You find yourself cheering and willing for that moment when the caterpillar will come out of the home as a moth. It will be Ba Ba. Everything will be okay again. You will find Ma Ma and you will all fly home upon his back, navigating by the pull of the moon.

With one last push, the creature pops out and climbs onto the window frame to stretch its crushed wings. You realize that it is not the big brown moth you thought it would be. It is a beautiful pale pink butterfly, almost translucent. As she moves her wings, now strong and fully outstretched, the frost on the window dissipates under her warmth and you can see your precious broken-down glasshouse outside.

The butterfly takes flight.

It is not your father. It is you.

She flits from the window and flutters around your head.

I will find my mother and get my mother the help she needs, you both think as one.

You float over to the wardrobe and the door opens. Pink plumes of smoke roll out like all the neon nightmares of your dreams. You step inside and a light comes on. Illuminated in front of you is a staircase.

Each step glows pink as you ascend, even though you don't touch them. You are light as air, a feather falling upward.

At the very top you don't find Big Scary's eye. Instead, lying on the ground, as big as the moon, in a round room completely covered in white sheeting, is Ma Ma.

You throw yourself down beside her.

Ma Ma, I love you.

She opens her eyes as your heart bursts into a million purple aster blossoms. You can read her mind and she tells you:

I found a place to hide.

Ma Ma sits up and cries out again and places her hand on her stomach.

I think the baby is coming.

You support Ma Ma with both your arms.

Ma Ma, I am here to carry you somewhere safe. I will tuck you into my heart, but don't worry about it being too cramped because my heart has never felt so big. Like you once carried me, I will carry you to safety.

You take the weight of Ma Ma tenderly on your

pink wings as the whole world dissolves around you, but you are not scared because all you have learned and all you have been through has made you strong, even though you are as fragile as a butterfly.

Down you fly over the staircase that used to be solid but is now only a memory.

The girl in you marches into the kitchen, the only room that is left.

Picking up the phone, you punch in three digits.

"Emergency services, can I help you?"

And you say, because the words finally manage to arrange themselves on your tongue:

"Please come quick. My family needs help."

You are a butterfly looking for a flower. You are a daughter looking out for your mother. You take her to the glasshouse, where it will be safe until help comes. The black-and-white gatekeeper lets you in, but then hurries off in alarm.

"Where am I?" asks Ma Ma as she opens her eyes and sees the millions of galaxies in the night sky. The moon smiles serenely and casts her silvery light.

"It's going to be okay," you tell her, and you squeeze her hand.

"I know," she says, trying to smile. "I know why I named you Meixing. Do you know what it means?"

Beautiful star.

"To me, you will always shine the brightest in the dark."

Her grip on your hand suddenly tightens until it is unbearable, but still you let her hang on and you don't pull away. Ma Ma places her other hand on her stomach and so do you. You can feel the life kicking inside her, wanting so much to live. With one final squeeze until all the tears pour down her face, Ma Ma gives it her all and your new baby sister comes open-eyed and crying into the world.

You look in wonder at the little pink newborn lying on Ma Ma's tummy. You pick her up oh so gently and the purple petals scattered upon her blow away in the wind. It is not until she touches your face with her tiny hand that you realize that tears are streaming down your face.

"I'm sorry there are so many things you've had to learn to adjust to," Ma Ma says, tears still falling from both eyes. "But your sister will grow up here and she will never know the pain you have known. This will always be her home."

The universe exhales and you can feel it.

"What are we going to name her?" you ask Ma Ma.

"How about Xinxing?" says Ma Ma. *New star.*

"And because she will always share part of the same

name as you, you will always be connected by the stars."

"I love her!" you exclaim. "I know I don't even know her yet, but I know I love her!"

You burst into tears, happy ones this time, and Ma Ma does too until you are a giddy and snotty pair.

"Thank you, Meixing. This hot-water bottle is keeping me nice and warm," says Ma Ma. Confused, you look down to see the pink serpent curled up against Ma Ma's side like some sort of pet.

You feel a hand on your shoulder. You look up to see First Uncle standing there smiling down at you. Standing there with him is . . .

"Ba Ba! You've finally come home!"

You look over at Ma Ma, but she doesn't seem to be able to see either of them.

"Meixing, look at you! I am so proud of how you have grown," says Ba Ba.

He holds out his hand, and you reach your hand over to him. Both your hands touch.

"Please look after your family," says Ba Ba as he looks fondly at Ma Ma and then tenderly at the baby in your arms. His eyes meet yours, and you feel yourself surrounded by so much love.

"It's time for us to go," First Uncle says. "Your father needs me to take him to his new life, and I think it's about time I began one of my own too. The glasshouse is yours now. I am completely confident that you will look after it and love it as much as I did."

He ruffles your hair affectionately.

You watch as First Uncle and Ba Ba slowly fade away until you can see the night sky through them. In one of the galaxies you believe you can see two new stars.

You feel a hand on your shoulder.

You look up and it is Kevin, with the black-and-white cat cradled and purring in his arms.

"I came as fast as I could. Is everyone safe?"

You nod and put your hand over his and hold on tightly.

Absolutely and completely, you know that your home is not anywhere else but here. With your family and your friends. There are flowers falling from the sky. They gently touch your face and you shed those butterfly wings and become yourself. Like a flower, you set your roots deep into the soil and feel yourself come to life and breathe and grow.

With your mind, you reach out to Big Scary and you rebuild her brick by brick and put her back together again. All her mismatched scales and her patchy fur and her funny moods and her inexact feelings, exactly how she is. Her perfectly imperfect self.

You look up at all the galaxies until your eyes become sore. Somewhere in the distance you can hear an ambulance siren wailing. The panes of the glasshouse flash in red and blue. Your imagination will always be there for you when you need it, to provide you solace and comfort, but now it is time for you to step back into reality. The colors in the panes of the glasshouse mix into each other and become purple.

You hand Xinxing back to Ma Ma and you go out to greet the paramedics.

What you notice first is that it's not so cold anymore.

Spring has arrived.

CHAPTER TWENTY-SIX

Rocket

It is the day of the big presentation, and Ms. Jardine's rickety classroom is bursting with special guests. Mr. and Mrs. Huynh are there and so is Kevin's grandmother, who is almost one hundred years old. You finally get to meet Josh's parents. Mrs. Khoury hands you a jar of olives to replace the one you lost and you take it shyly; she asks you to come over for dinner sometime and you tell her you would love to.

You stand shoulder to shoulder with Kevin and Josh, a little nervous, a little excited, crowded around the food table Ms. Jardine has set up, stuffing potato chips into your mouths. You look at the audience as they take their seats, and it is almost time for the three of you to take the stage.

Josh goes first. He reads the story about Book Boy, and the more he reads, the more powerful his hero becomes. He trips up villains with his vast knowledge; banishes baddies by being much smarter than all of them. Book Boy can't be contained, as he knows every way to escape and how to read every situation. He has his trusty sidekicks, one of them being Grammatical Girl, who is very strict about sentence structure and has the ability to shift time from the past to the present tense. She is also a very good and kind friend. Then there is also Drawing Dude, whose every sketch becomes reality and who is very useful for drawing holes and scissors or whatever the situation calls for, but he's bad at reading maps.

Everyone claps and cheers. Josh blushes and goes to sit with his parents.

Kevin goes next, and he has written a fairy tale, except instead of a prince saving a princess or even a princess saving a prince, it is about a boy and a girl who can take care of themselves (thank you very much), helping each other to carry on. They go on grand adventures on a long wooden boat that sails through the night sky to different planets and stars in the galaxy, visiting alien races and running away from space monsters. They even spend an extended stint on Europa, the water moon, for under the ice crust is a whole ocean of extraterrestrial life to explore, but they are happy in the end to return home to planet Earth.

There is loud clapping and cheering, especially from Kevin's hundred-year-old grandmother. Kevin pretends to be bashful by looking at the floor and kicking at it, but his ears have turned red. He is secretly pleased.

Then it is your turn to step up on the stage to tell your story, and your story goes:

"I live in a house called Big Scary, even though she is not always scary. Sometimes she is kind. She is more than a house, she is our home.

"Big Scary has one eye that lives in the very top room. There is only one way to get there and it is a secret. Inside the room, once all the sheets are removed, is a library full of all sorts of books. One day I hope to be able to read all of them. Right now I can only read the simple books, but one day I will be able to read the ones with really big words.

"When Big Scary is feeling sad, she shrinks. When she is happy, there is no limit to how big she can get. I have realized she is only a reflection of ourselves. She is not perfect, but she is only human. In fact, I am thinking of changing her name to Little Scary.

"I have a magical greenhouse in the backyard that is filled with magic seeds of imagination. You only need to plant them for ideas to grow. I go there when I'm feeling sad. I'm not scared when it gets dark inside, as that's when the stars shine the brightest. Maybe one day I won't need to go there anymore, but I hope that I always need to dream. Even when I'm an adult.

"Although there are challenges in life, everyone lived happily ever after."

You have tried not to look at the audience all this time because you are still nervous, but mainly because you are afraid you will be overcome with emotions and you won't be able to keep reciting. Now that everyone is giving you the biggest claps and cheers for going last, you cast your eyes upward.

You see Mr. and Mrs. Huynh smiling at you.

You see Mr. and Mrs. Khoury giving you a standing ovation.

You see Ms. Jardine beaming so hard.

You see Mr. Jones patting her on the shoulder.

You see Kevin and Josh giving you the thumbs-up.

You see Ma Ma, with Xinxing sleeping tucked against her body inside a stretchy cloth like a pink cocoon.

And you see Ailing. Who you now call Aunty Ailing so that she knows she will always be wanted, now that she lives in an apartment up the street from Little Scary. Ma Ma makes her *kueh* and Ailing gives her too much in return for them, but you know Ailing wants to make sure Ma Ma has enough money. Ma Ma talks about opening a *kueh* stall one day to provide for you all. Ailing cried when you invited her to your presentation day. Now her eyes crinkle again as she fights back happy tears.

Last but not least, you see yourself. You realize there are tears rolling down your face too, but you let them roll because they are tears of hope.

You step off the stage, and Kevin and Josh both engulf you in a huge hug.

You think about the fun you will have on the weekend exploring the glasshouse and Little Scary together. You will show them the pale pink door that has suddenly come back on the second floor. The one behind which you once saw a rocket ship, a slide, and a spinning wheel.

You have never felt as much as you do right now that you truly belong.

Acknowledgments

Foremost to my agent, Gemma Cooper, who was first to say, "I believe in you," and is the lighthouse who guides me through the dark. Jessica Townsend for being my unofficial talent scout! My three wonderful editors, Zoe Walton, Rebecca Hill, and Krista Vitola, who helped lift me to even greater heights—go Team ZoBecSta! Becky Walker for the invaluable extra guidance and the cheering from the sidelines. Thank you to Jillian Nguyen and Rawah Arja for being my authenticity readers and offering me their valuable insight. The three other members of "The Faux Four"—Cristy Burne, H. M. Waugh, and Nadia L. King—for being authors and understanding. Kim Wisniewski, for putting up with my fully baby temper tantrums and being there for this long. Jacob Rechner, for unexpectedly teaching me how to write so simple and clean. Thuan Vo, for sharing with me his personal family story. Finally, to my sister, Leena Mah Vo, for being my first reader and the glue that holds everything together; she is truly made of stars.